THE DEVIL YOU KNOW

Also by Jenn Farrell

Sugar Bush & Other Stories

The Devil You Know

STORIES

Jenn Farrell

Anvil Press | Vancouver

Anvil Press Publishers Inc.
P.O. Box 3008, Main Post Office
Vancouver, B.C. V6B 3X5 Canada
www.anvilpress.com

Library and Archives Canada Cataloguing in Publication

Farrell, Jenn
The devil you know / Jenn Farrell.

Short stories.
ISBN 978-1-897535-06-6

I. Title.

PS8611.A774D48 2010   C813'.6   C2010-904207-X

Printed and bound in Canada
Cover design by Mutasis Creative
Cover art by Katie Pretti
Author photo: Wendy D
Interior design by HeimatHouse

Represented in Canada by the Literary Press Group
Distributed by the University of Toronto Press

The publisher gratefully acknowledges the financial assistance of the Canada
Council for the Arts, the Canada Book Fund, and the Province of British
Columbia through the B.C. Arts Council and the Book Publishing Tax Credit.

for
Ailsa, Amy, Elise, Joan, and Wendy

CONTENTS

SAM FOUND THE CAR KEYS ON THE HOOK BY THE FRONT DOOR and drove her mother's rusty Accord straight to the hospital. She gave her name at the reception desk and waited for a social worker named Elise to take her down to the morgue. Elise walked with Sam to the elevator and unlocked their floor with a keycard. They went down, into the basement of the hospital, the part without gift shops or cafeterias. Elise pressed a buzzer on the wall; a young man poked his head out a doorway, nodded, went back inside, and then opened another door down the hall a few moments later. Sam walked into what looked like a small waiting room, painted pale yellow and fluorescently lit. There were soft chairs and a couch and a coffee table with a box of tissues and an open doorway to a green tiled room in the centre of which sat a stainless steel gurney with her dead mother on it. Sam dropped her purse on the coffee table and walked through the doorway.

Day of the Dead

Sam didn't immediately recognize the shape of the body under the white sheet. The cancer had stripped more than half her mother's bulk away, but her middle was bloated with the fluid they had been draining off every few days. Her shoulders and head were exposed and Sam noticed how small and bony she seemed. For the first time, Sam could see the resemblance between her mother and her grandmother.

The hair on her mother's head had thinned, and hadn't been cut or permed for some time. It hung back from her forehead, limp and white. Her facial hair had been neglected too, her chin hairs and moustache growing in.

"Oh, Mom," Sam said. "You look terrible." If she had come sooner, she could have at least cleaned her up a bit.

Her mother's sunken face did not radiate peace, or even rest. The last few days of her life must have been an ugly fight. Sam tried to touch her mother, mostly because she thought that's what people were supposed to do, but she couldn't bring her trembling hand into contact. She hovered over her ruined hair, her face, and noted the absence of warmth. One of her eyelids was not completely closed, and Sam peered into the sliver of visible eye. It seemed to look back at her, baleful. Judging.

"I'm sorry I wasn't here, okay?" she whispered. "I fucked up."

Sam said other things too, things she was barely aware of saying aloud, but she could hear herself crying and the sound of the social worker crying behind her and the whirring of the cooling fans. She realized that this would be the last memory she had of the woman, that this body on a gurney would now be the picture she saw when she thought of her mother, and that there would be no new last memory to replace it.

A thin stream of greenish-black fluid began to run out of her mother's nose and towards the opening of her ear and Sam watched its progression, transfixed, horrified. The social worker appeared at her side and dabbed her dead mother's face with a tissue. Then she offered one to Sam, and they turned and left the room.

❀ ❀ ❀

The cemetery office building was frigid compared to the shimmering midday asphalt of the parking lot. Sam lifted her hair and exposed her neck to the cold air blowing through a floor vent beside the reception desk. She was no longer used to the heat, the Southern Ontario humidity that was like breathing through a hot wet rag. Sam's shorts clung to the backs of her damp thighs and wrinkled in the front, and she wished she had worn a skirt.

The front desk was unoccupied, but a tiny man in a suit and tie appeared through a doorway and smiled at her. Sam was getting used to all the suits, a prerequisite for dealing with the dead, regardless of the heat.

"You must be Samantha," he said. His hand, when she shook it, was nearly as small as her own. *Petite*, Sam thought. Even the bones of his face looked delicate, almost elfin. He introduced himself as Michael, the Services Director. She liked how the title rang with professional anonymity; a label that wouldn't make people squirm, like *undertaker* might.

"Sam, please. Only my mother called me Samantha."

As he led her into the office, she noticed that his salt-and-pepper hair was thick but wanted cutting, with that long shagginess in the back that she hated. Sometimes her clients wanted to leave that length, especially if they were thinning on top and believed that longer hair in the back made up for it. Sam was usually able to convince them otherwise. The advice of an attractive woman carried some weight in matters of hairstyle.

Michael's office was filled with shelves displaying urns, memorial plaques, and granite headstone samples. Sam examined a wooden display with a number of necklaces hanging from it and fingered a heart-shaped pendant as though she were in a shop. A small brass plaque explained that the "memory pendants" were meant to be filled with loved one's ashes. She let go of the heart and it rapped against the wood.

"So," Michael said, sitting across the desk and interlocking his wee hands neatly, "I understand you're here today to discuss your mother's arrangements. I'm so sorry for your loss."

There had been as many apologies as there had been suits. "These things happen," she said, opening her palms to the ceiling. "But this, um…arrangement has made it a bit easier." Through a typical Williams family screw-up, a plot purchased by her grandfather in the '50s had gone unclaimed. Some great aunt had married a Jewish guy fifty years ago and left her eternal Presbyterian resting place vacant. It was Uncle Clifford who had tried to give Sam all the information right there in the arrivals area of the airport, before she'd even pulled her luggage off the carousel.

"Give me a fucking minute, wouldya?" she'd snapped, her fellow travellers' faces wide-eyed. Even the top of Clifford's old-man head had blushed. Sam tried to make polite conversation during the ride home, but the damage was done. He wouldn't even get out of the car when he dropped her off. One major family insult accomplished before she'd even seen her mother's body.

"—and since that facility is a member of our larger family of funeral services providers, the transfer of ownership is a relatively simple process—with the necessary forms of course." Michael presented Sam with a series of papers to be signed and initialled, which she did with a suitably heavy ballpoint pen.

"Let's move on," said Michael, "to your mother's wishes. Did she leave you any instructions at all?"

"Well, my mother wanted to be cremated and then have her remains thrown into the trash. She was always a bit of a drama queen that way. But even though I'm going to totally ignore her and her stupid wishes, I'd like to keep things as simple as possible."

Michael scarcely flinched, but Sam felt satisfied by her own testiness. It felt good to have her personality back for a minute, after all the polite whispering of the past few days. The obligatory visits to the airless sitting rooms of her few remaining relatives made her want to scream, but sitting home alone was even worse. An air-conditioned audience with Mr. Services Director was something of an improvement over both.

He flipped through a binder of plastic sheets, keeping up the sales patter as he went. There were many things to decide: the urn, interment in the ground or a crypt (which Michael called a memorial wall), matters of size, shape, colour…Sam was baffled by the array of choices for the dead. Whatever she chose, it would most certainly not be in accordance with the note she had found in her mother's safety deposit box that morning.

"My Wishes"
My death is to be followed by cremation
If it's put in the paper, do it after the fact (I mean later)
(No service! Or memorial service NO PICTURES)

Ashes in a cardboard box only
Given to my daughter to be thrown in the garbage
WON'T COST MUCH AND NO TIME SPENT
You do not have the right to judge or change these wishes
*   NO FLOWERS—IN LIEU OF—Charitable donations to children's char-*
ities of your choice. The children are the future—help them!
*   Hooray the witch is dead!*
*   Signed by, A Misfit*

The note was not a surprise. Sam's mother had been working over that particular turf for years. She'd brought up one variation or another of those instructions so frequently, and with such bitterness, that Sam had always thought she'd have no trouble following them. She had often pictured herself walking out of some funeral home with her purse over her shoulder, a grande Starbucks cup in one hand, and a white cardboard box in the other. *Fuck you, you got your wish,* she would say, lobbing the box into the first garbage can she passed on the sidewalk. But now that she was actually dead, Sam was puzzled to discover that a lot of her mother's bullshit had died with her. Their fights that had gone on for years suddenly ended, even if Sam hadn't been finished fighting them yet.

In addition to not wanting to throw what was left of her mother into the trash, Sam discovered that she had no desire to hold a box of human ashes. She remembered how at the hospital she couldn't even touch her mother's body, that creepy cold shell that had nearly nothing to do with the person she had known. The idea of keeping the ashes, or wearing a pinch of them in a special pendant, was sickening.

She had called the newspaper and arranged for a small notice to appear in the Saturday obituaries after everything had been completed. There would be no funeral, no memorial service, but at least there would be a place to visit if anyone wanted. If the plot hadn't been an almost-freebie, things might have gone differently. Real estate costs were high, even underground. But this way, the body had travelled straight from the hospital to the funeral home, and then would go on to the crematorium and the cemetery, all without Sam having to touch anything more than pieces of paper.

Sam flipped through the selection of urns and chose a plain, white marble vessel shaped like a tall shoebox, not at all like what she thought of as an urn. One of their most economical options, it cost six hundred dollars. She imagined the box being sealed behind a wall, like a coffin in an Egyptian tomb, never to be seen again. "How do I know that you actually use this and don't just put the ashes in another box and keep this one to sell again?" she asked.

"Most of our families do attend the interment and have a small service or say a few words at that time, Miss Black." Michael was proving to be unflappable. Sam reminded herself to pronounce it "interment" instead of "internment."

He showed her a photocopied map of the grounds and the locations of various plots. Sam thought the ground was a nicer place to be than a big marble mausoleum with everyone's boxes all jammed in together. "Would you like to take a walk around?" he asked. "It's very warm out, but it might give you a better idea of some of the available options."

As they crossed the parking lot together, Sam resisted an unexpected desire to take Michael's hand. The last few days had brought unwieldy and confusing feelings to the surface. At first, she'd had no appetite, and there was a shiver of delight that cut through her numbness. Could this grief burn its way through five or ten pounds? The answer came the next afternoon, when she ate half a jar of marshmallow fluff from her mother's fridge because it was one of the few things that hadn't expired. And now, all day, she'd been aching for physical contact with someone—no matter how stupid the circumstance—even this small-handed man in a suit. She had brushed against the hand of the gas-station attendant when he passed her her credit card slip that morning, and the urge to wrap herself around him had almost made her cry with longing.

As they walked, Michael gestured at a giant white Jesus with outstretched arms at the top of a slight incline. "That area there is our Garden of Grace," he said, "and behind that is our Walk of Memory. Most of those spaces are pre-booked, however," he said, meeting her eyes. "A very popular option nowadays."

Sam just nodded, busy thinking of other good names. The Path of Righteousness? The Valley of the Shadow of Death? The Road to Nowhere?

They followed the winding pavement to a pond surrounded by benches and memorial columns. On the other side of the pond stood a decent-sized maple. Sam pointed at its base. "Over there," she said. "Is that a spot?"

Michael consulted his laminated map. "Yes, Plot 256. It's very nice, but it's right beside the roadway. Some people like to be a little further away. If you've got elderly relatives, however, it's easy to find and there's not much walking to do..."

Sam walked towards it. The tree made a small blob of shade, and the grass looked a little thicker and less thirsty there. "She hated the sun," she said. "She'd be pissed if I put her in direct sunlight." She turned to Michael. "It gave her hives, that's why she hated it. I think this is the one."

The plot chosen, they headed back towards the main building. A hot breeze ruffled Sam's hair and made strings of it stick to her face and chest. She pulled them away with her fingers and saw Michael looking at the wide vee of her shirt, her tan and freckled collarbones against the white of the cotton.

Back inside, Michael passed her a binder full of designs for the bronze plaque that would mark the gravesite. It was easy enough to choose something small and basic, with a border of roses. Her mother had liked flowers. It struck Sam as odd that she had been so against them in her note. Then Sam needed to choose a sentiment of some kind to put on the plaque, and Michael produced a helpful pamphlet with biblical phrases and snippets of poems. "Of course, you're welcome to come up with something on your own, if you prefer," he said.

Thin at last? she thought. Or how about *I told you I was sick*? She pinched the inside of her bottom lip with her incisor to keep from smirking. She pretended to be overwhelmed and asked to use the ladies' room.

The bathroom had its own aircon vent and was even cooler than the rest of the office. Sam looked in the mirror, running her hands over her white shirt. Even rumpled and sweaty, she looked too good to be pissing the day away in a funeral parlour, or whatever this place was supposed to be called. She leaned forward and rested her forehead against the cool of the mirror for a moment. It left a greasy print.

"I think I have to go," she said to Michael when she returned.

He clucked sympathetically. "Of course. It can be a lot to take in all at once. Take this with you," he said, handing her the pamphlet. He had already stapled his business card to its front. "When you've selected something, just give me a call." He placed his hand on her shoulder and Sam nearly let a sob escape. She turned away to keep herself from collapsing into his arms.

Sam drove to the convenience store and loaded up on supplies: Diet Coke, chips, chocolate bars, Frosted Flakes, fashion magazines, and a carton of Belmont Milds. There was almost nothing to eat in her mother's house: the cancer took her hunger, something Sam never thought she'd see. It had been over a year since Sam had been in the house, but it looked like no new food had come in since then. The kitchen cupboards held only expired boxes and dusty cans: packets of instant diet pudding, cake mixes, low-fat soups, sugar-free iced tea mix. Sam mostly ate sushi and brown rice and lattes and fruit smoothies from the shops near the hair salon. But here in the aisles of the mini-mart, she surrendered to the lure of the child food in its shiny, rainbow packages. Even chips and pop were better than what she'd be purging from the old woman's cupboards.

Back at the house, Sam cracked a Diet Coke and was about to go out on the porch for a smoke when she realized that the house belonged to her now, and so she lit a cigarette sitting at the kitchen table. She read the pamphlet of quotes. Most of the passages were embarrassing and trite, or too religious, or sounded desperate, things that made Sam think of people draping their weeping selves over coffins. She finally decided to go with the last line of Browning's Sonnet 43, "I shall but love thee better after death." Stripped of its context, the line was awkward, sounding almost like "I like you better now that you're dead," which she understood. Her mother was definitely easier to get along with now. She rolled a joint on the placemat.

The thought of actually cleaning out the entire house was daunting. Every closet, cupboard, and drawer needed to be emptied, its contents evaluated and inevitably discarded. Clothes and furniture and accumulated piles of useless crap: *Reader's Digest* condensed books from the '60s, worn-out orthopedic shoes, a man's overcoat that Sam didn't recognize, at least a garbage bag's worth of empty pill bottles, and a set of Funk and Wagnalls encyclopedias that her mother had collected using grocery-store stamps and had been so proud of…there would be carloads of stuff to take to Value Village. Sam reminded herself that it didn't have to happen at all once. Maybe she could recruit a couple of old high-school girlfriends who still lived in the area. She knew them from their Facebook pages, now wives and mothers, raising their own families in the neighbourhoods they used to prowl on drunken Saturday nights. She could call them, and they would help her out. It might even be fun to see them again.

Bolstered by her own pep talk and a few puffs of the joint, Sam decided to take another look around. The hallway closet seemed the least visibly packed; a relatively safe place to start. There were some old liquor bottles on the top shelf, and Sam pulled down a bottle of cherry whisky she recognized from childhood. It looked drinkable. Beside the bottles were stacks of photo albums, picture frames, and a few floral-print boxes meant for storing photographs. Sam ground the crusty lid from the whisky and carried the boxes into the living room. They did hold photos, mostly, along with clippings from newspapers and magazines: mostly comic strips, Ann Landers columns, and quasi-religious inspirational passages. On the top of the pile in the third box, Sam found a note addressed to her on a piece of kitten-bordered paper.

To Samantha

Remember, If you feel any guilt at all—try denial! It works for some people!

You never made time for a meaningful conversation or had any TIME for me!! All I was to you was the slave who tried to make home a home.

I believed! And I cared! And you turned your back to me.

Sam turned the note over.

I have to admire greatly the strength of anyone who can turn their life around after making ALL the wrong choices. When people start making adult choices—supposedly they are an adult. We are all humans and not perfect—there's no such thing.

I've since learned that if you start working with a young child and their choices, not an adult's, they will learn by their mistakes and not be as devastated by their errors or by adult choices pushed on them. Small child—small choices, and by the time you're older the decisions made may not be so traumatic even if they ARE wrong.

We were raised in the era where you went out and made your own way, and your own place to sleep, and you didn't blame anyone else for your lot in life.

The actress and the melodrama are all that come first for you and always will be.

I'm just glad you didn't end up on a pig farm in B.C.

"Jesus Christ." Sam took a long pull of the whisky. It tasted like cough syrup. "I cut hair, for fucksakes."

❋   ❋   ❋

Sam awoke on the couch with the detritus of the previous night all around her: the cherry whisky bottle on the coffee table, photos and bits of paper scattered around the carpet. She had been unable to face sleeping in her mother's bed.

Her loneliness felt like a garment around her, and Sam turned on the radio to try and shake it off, along with her headache. She craved good coffee and good music, but knew she'd find neither. She wished she'd thought more about what to pack; she could have brought some coffee beans, her iPod, and a blow dryer. As it was, she'd swept the contents of her bathroom counter into one suitcase, and into another she'd thrown shorts and T-shirts, along with a couple of black skirts and dresses, since she'd been fairly certain she'd need a funeral outfit eventually. She had been in the cab on the way to the airport, trying to imagine tearful, heartfelt goodbyes at the bedside, trying to picture all the things that she and her mother had never managed to pull off in life now coming naturally to both of them, when her cell phone rang, telling her she was already too late. She was two for two now, if anyone was keeping score on missing the death of parent. Sam hadn't made it to her father's passing either, when he was crushed between two train cars at the steel mill a month before her birth.

Sam ate a bag of ketchup chips for breakfast and called Michael. He suggested that she come in at ten-thirty, and although she had planned to just tell him the Browning line over the phone, she agreed. Sam thought about what to wear while she showered. She decided on her yellow sundress with the cap sleeves, even though she sometimes worried that it was too young for her. When she climbed into the Accord, she felt excited, as though she were going to meet a lover.

Sam pulled into the parking lot beside the silver Acura that must have belonged to Michael. Getting out, she bent down to check her lip gloss in the Acura's passenger window and noticed something hanging in the back window. She moved closer, shielding her eyes from the glare. It was a shirt or jacket in a drycleaning bag. The silky green fabric and big gold buttons reminded her of a Renaissance costume, or a pirate. The cuffs of matching knickers or pantaloons hung beneath the shirt's hem. Resting on the back seat was a long black nylon bag. Gun, sword, musical instrument? Sam stood and hastily buffed the window with the hem of her dress to remove her hand prints.

This time, a trim brunette sat at the reception desk. Her pretty eyes peered at Sam over the tops of glasses a decade out of fashion. "Michael is on the phone, but he'll be with you in a moment," she said. Sam fussed with her ponytail, picked at her cuticles. When the brunette's phone beeped, she picked it up and gave Sam a nod. Sam walked in and sat in the same seat as she had before.

"How are you today, Sam?"

"Um, I think I've picked something out." She released the sweaty pamphlet from her hand, smoothed it out on the desk, and pointed to the number she'd circled. To her surprise, Michael recited the last few lines of the sonnet in a buttery voice.

I love thee with a love I seemed to lose
With my lost saints,—I love thee with the breath,
Smiles, tears, of all my life!—and, if God choose,
I shall but love thee better after death.

Sam nodded.

"Are you fond of poetry?" he asked.

"I'm a hair stylist."

"The language of love," he said, "is accessible to all of us."

She nodded again, staring at his hair. She imagined standing behind him, fastening the vinyl hairstyling cape around his neck, reclining him at the shampoo sink, the water and suds flowing through her fingers.

Michael cleared his throat and moved his fingertips together. "Sam, I want to ask you something rather serious," he said, leaning forward and looking into her eyes.

She didn't mean for the "yes" to escape as a whisper, but it did.

"Have you given any consideration," he said, "to your own arrangements when the time comes?"

"Arrangements...sorry, what?" Sam tried to translate his words into what she'd expected to hear.

Michael waited, then spoke again. "It's just that, now that there's already a plot here for your mother, we can offer you quite a reasonable rate for your own, especially with our interest-free prepayment plans. Many of our clients find that this alleviates a lot of unnecessary worry. Of course," he said, watching Sam's face, "if it's too soon to discuss these matters, I completely understand."

She barked out a laugh. "I thought you were about to ask me out." She looked down at herself, sitting in a budget office chair, her purse between her ankles, dressed like a girl going to a birthday party.

❋ ❋ ❋

Sam ground the gears as she pulled out of the parking lot, glancing back at the silver Acura in the rearview mirror. Michael and his receptionist-wife were probably standing together and watching her drive away, his small hands a perfect fit around her small shoulders.

There had been a long pause as she looked at her feet before Michael asked if she should perhaps come another day when she was feeling better. She had laughed again, but it sounded ridiculous, like a donkey. He told her what day her mother's remains would be interred and she remembered saying that she wouldn't be attending and that there would be no service. His expression had telegraphed pity, and she had stood up, noticed the slim gold band on his finger for the first time, and retreated from the office to her car.

The ride home passed in the blur of familiar houses, with the same sad, dry brown grass all around. Sam pulled into the driveway without checking the mailbox, turned off the car, and hurried into the house. She flipped on the radio tuned to an insipid oldies station and lit the remains of the previous night's joint. When it was gone, she walked into the bathroom and rummaged through her makeup bag. She removed her haircutting scissors and grabbed her ponytail with her free hand. She started by snipping away at the ends, but gradually worked her way up, where the scissors began to resist the thick hank of hair. She squeezed the hair flat and kept cutting. The cuttings fell around her feet, landing on her sandals and toes. Sam slid the elastic off the ponytail's stump and shook her hair out. It was uneven, but it could still be fixed if she stopped. A chin-length bob. She kept cutting. She held out random sections and cut each down nearly to the scalp until there was almost nothing left. Haphazard longer pieces stood on end and contrasted with her darker roots, giving the impression of a broken doll or a sickly orphan. Sam set the scissors on the counter and ran her hands over her patchy head. The woman in the mirror looked naked, skull-like. Sam saw her grandmother's cheekbones, her mother's baleful eye. She saw her own emptiness, her heart so open, so capable of love, and not a soul in the world to give it to. This was her house now. This was her life now. And, somewhere, a hole in the earth waited for her.

THE VAN CRESTED THE LAST OF THE BIG HILLS, AND ALTHOUGH
Ginny couldn't yet see the cabin, she knew by the look of relief on her
mother's face that they were nearly there. Forests lined the road, and
the sun shone between the spruce trees in bright stripes that reminded
Ginny of the pictures in her book of Bible stories. Although they had
only been driving for a day, their early morning departure seemed to
have been ages ago: the loading of their bags in the still-dark, and Ginny
slipping her boots and her jacket on over her pajamas. They had made
it across the state line into Pennsylvania, through Erie, then Warren,
and then up and up into the
Allegheny Mountains.

"Pass my smokes, baby,"
said Debby, her mother. Debby
had wedged her lighter into a
split in the sun-scorched plastic of the console, but the Virginia Slims pack still slid
across the dash with every
turn. Ginny pulled her bum

Solitaire

forward in her seat and grasped the cigarettes from her side of the van. She
loved the Virginia Slims packs and had been collecting them for a few
months. Every time her mother was finished one, Ginny neatly cut out the
package's floral border and kept them in one of her father's old cigar
boxes. She hadn't yet figured out what to do with them all, but sometimes
she used one as a bookmark.

"Mama?"

"Yes, you can have that one too."

"No, Mama. I want to know—will Grandma and Grandpa be there?"

"I already told you, baby. It's Thanksgiving. They always go to the
cabin at Thanksgiving."

Ginny knew Mama couldn't call them to tell them the surprise news
that they were coming, because there wasn't a phone at the cabin. Be-

sides, her mother had thrown her cell phone out the window hours ago, right off the bridge into the Roanoke River.

The cabin was still there on the right, in a row of weather-beaten holiday cottages and mobile homes. Everything looked exactly as it had when Ginny visited three years before. Debby backed the van into the strip of weedy brown grass beside the cabin, and Ginny jumped out and stood in the yard, smelling wood smoke and crunchy spruce needles. Mama took Ginny's hand as they climbed the porch steps.

The kitchen was filled with steam. Ginny's grandmother looked up from stirring a big silver pot on the stove.

"Grandma!" Ginny yelled.

"Oh, my sweetie," said Grandma, and opened her arms wide, as though no time had gone by at all.

"Debby," Grandma said as she squeezed Ginny with her soft fat arms. "Why didn't you tell us you were coming?"

"Hi Mama. Thought we'd come up and have Thanksgiving with y'all, if you don't mind. Ginny missed you something awful."

"Is that so?" said Grandma. She held her Ginny out in front of her. "Did you miss your Grandma?"

"I did miss you, Grandma, and Grandpa too."

Grandpa's voice boomed from the doorway between the kitchen and living room. "Is that my baby girl or am I gone crackers?"

"Grandpa!" Ginny flung herself at his huge belly and let him mess up her hair, while the two women talked behind them in quiet voices. She knew they were talking about Dwayne, where he was and why he wasn't with them. She hoped Mama wasn't getting in trouble.

"Mama and me left this morning before Dwayne even woke up," Ginny whispered to her grandfather.

"Let's you and me go sit outside for a while then."

She heard her grandmother say, "I could have told you that years ago, saved you the trouble," but didn't hear her mother's reply as the screen door swung shut.

Ginny and Grandpa Joe sat at the picnic table on the back porch. Ginny could sometimes hardly remember what her father's face looked like before he got sick, or the sound of his voice, but the back porch brought back her memory. The smell of stale cigar smoke, the soft flapping sound of the plastic enclosing the porch, the vinyl tablecloth marked with stains and burns. She could remember her father here, before the hospital, sitting and drinking and talking with Grandpa in his white undershirt. She remembered Daddy's plaid shirt tucked into his green work pants, and the package of White Owl cigars peeking out of his shirt pocket. Sometimes men from the other cabins came over, or aunts and uncles drove up in their RVs, and the men would play cards and drink beers from the blue Coleman cooler while the women made Thanksgiving dinner. When there weren't enough men for a game, Daddy and Grandpa taught Ginny how to play Go Fish and Crazy Eights and Solitaire. Grandpa had even given Ginny her own deck of cards to practise with. And she took the cards home with her and played Solitaire all the time, especially when her father got too sick to play with her. She'd lay the cards out on his wheelie hospital tray while her mother sat beside him and touched his face. When Ginny got bored of playing Solitaire, she'd lay the face cards out and decide which ones were her favourites. She liked the Queen of Clubs, because her hair was the longest, and because she had a little smile. She wished the Queen of Hearts was the prettiest one, but she looked sideways with scared eyes and a sad mouth.

On the day Daddy died, Ginny put a hair elastic around her cards and placed them in the bottom drawer with the too-small nightgowns and the woolly winter socks. Mama kept her home from school. Ginny followed her mother around the house whenever she got out of bed, putting out all the cigarettes she left burning in ashtrays, just like Grandma had told her to do. Then Grandma said it was time to go back to school, and she came over every day at breakfast and made waffles and porridge and packed Ginny's lunch with bologna sandwiches and made macaroni and cheese for dinner and gave her a Coca-Cola if she was a good girl. Debby drifted from her bed to the kitchen table to the bed again, like a ghost in a pink bathrobe.

❋　❋　❋

After they had brought the bags in from the van and eaten dinner, Grandpa asked Ginny if she wanted to go looking for deer. Grandpa was too old and tired and fat to go out deer hunting anymore, so now he just liked to go for a drive at night and look at them. Grandpa's pickup truck was so high off the ground Ginny had to be lifted into the cab. Grandpa eased the truck down the road while she held the giant flashlight, its face a glowing moon that lit a path deep into the woods, making eerie night-time shadows in the trees. After a few minutes they spotted a doe and her fawn, caged in the mesmerizing beam. Their eyes glittered green, and they were so close Ginny could see the flesh and fur twitching along the tops of their flanks. As the truck inched forward, they leapt into the air, white tails flashing, and vanished into the trees as the light passed over them.

"There's a buck," whispered Grandpa, pointing ahead on his side of the truck. As if he knew what they had come for, the buck strode onto the road and into the headlights. His neck was long and muscular and swollen from the rut, his antlers wide and rubbed nearly clean of their velvet. He sauntered across the road, seemingly aware of his own beauty, and down into the ditch on the other side.

Ginny counted twenty-three deer. It never occurred to her that she might have counted some of the same ones twice. She believed she could tell them all apart. All that night she dreamt of chasing them, their delicate hooves and flashing tails always just beyond her reach.

❋　❋　❋

The next morning, Grandma made blueberry pancakes for breakfast and Ginny ate five with syrup and sausages.

"Keep eating like that and you'll be as big as me one day," said Grandpa, patting his round belly.

"Leave her alone, Dad."

"He's just making a joke, Debby. Don't be so keyed up. Anyways, we can all see she's just a tiny thing, aren't you, dear?"

"She's got a bony butt, that's for sure," said her mother.

Grandma cleared the table and handed Debby a list. "You and your father have to go to the store for supplies if I'm going to make a decent Thanksgiving dinner. I was only planning for the two of us. I think I've got a big enough turkey, but I need more corn and potatoes and yams…well, you've got the list."

"Oh, Mom…" Debby sounded like one of Ginny's fourth-grade class-mates. "Can't we go later?"

"No, you cannot. I want you in that store before they sell every Brus-sels sprout and can of cranberry sauce in the place. Ginny can stay and help me a get a start on things."

❋   ❋   ❋

After Grandma had shooed Debby and Joe out of the house, she put the kettle on for hot chocolate and sat down at the kitchen table with Ginny.

"Sweetie, do you remember how your mama met Dwayne?"

Ginny remembered. It was a few months after Daddy died, when Mama got a job as a checkout girl at the Piggly Wiggly. "He asked her out when she was ringing up his groceries," said Ginny.

"I never wanted you to go away, Ginny. I want you to understand that," she said, taking her hand and looking intently at her. "Your grandpa and I were so sad when you left and we wondered if we'd ever get to see you again."

When Dwayne and Mama had been dating for a while, and Dwayne had been staying over a lot, Debby sat Ginny down at the kitchen table for a talk that seemed grownup and serious, like this one did. She told her that when Daddy died, their house wasn't finished being paid for, and she couldn't afford to pay the rest on her own. Debby told Ginny that Dwayne wanted to go back to Virginia, where he could get a good job, and that he wanted Mama and Ginny to go with him. All Ginny knew about Virginia was that it was for lovers.

The new house in Virginia wasn't as nice as the old house in Pennsylvania, but Mama told Ginny not to complain, especially to Dwayne. It was small and a little bit falling apart in places, but Ginny had her own room and the family across the road had a tire swing in their front yard with a big pile of hay you could jump into. Dwayne started his new job driving truck, and was mostly gone just for a day at a time. Sometimes he did a longer trip, and then he'd come back with a chocolate bar or a T-shirt for Ginny and a carton of cigarettes for Mama. Dwayne told funny stories, getting up from the kitchen table to act out the different parts and making Ginny laugh even if she didn't want to. Mama told her they were very lucky to have found a good man like Dwayne. Ginny still missed her Daddy though. Even though Dwayne was funny and nice, Daddy had seemed to make her mother more calm, more sure of what she was doing. Without him, she sometimes seemed to drift away, not finishing her sentences or just staring at nothing for a while with a scared look in her eyes, like she might bolt if you made any sudden movements.

They had been living in Virginia for about a year when Dwayne got in his accident. He got some money from his work, but he couldn't sit behind the wheel all day or lift heavy things anymore. He stayed home and watched television because the pain medicine he took made him tired and cranky, then he started drinking to cheer himself up. Dwayne turned into a different person when he drank, but not like when a normal person turns into a superhero. Instead of saving people from fires and bad guys, Dwayne turned into a person who threw dishes and stood yelling in the front yard in his underpants. Sometimes it would seem funny to Ginny, almost like he was telling one of his stories, but other times it was scary. Ginny worried about Mama, who would sometimes yell back at him and sometimes cry and hide in the bathroom and other times would pull Ginny by the arm to the van and drive away. They usually went to

McDonald's for a couple of hours and Mama drank coffee and Ginny could play in the ball room for as long as she wanted.

Once a week Mama would call Grandma and Grandpa, and Ginny would get to talk to them, but only after she'd promised not to say anything about Dwayne.

Sometimes Ginny would get out her old deck of cards and lay them out on her bed and make up stories. She would be the Queen of Clubs, who was so smart and brave that she used all of her clubs to rescue the sad Queen of Hearts from the Jack of Spades. Then the two Queens went to a witch, who sent them back in time to live happily ever after in a castle with the King of Hearts, who had been away for a long time but hadn't died after all.

✳ ✳ ✳

Before they had moved away, Debby and Grandma argued a lot—sometimes on the phone and sometimes in person. When Grandma came over to argue, Ginny was supposed to sit in her room and listen to the radio. Ginny would do as she was told, but she'd lie on the floor with her ear at the space under the door and try to make out the words. Ginny was glad her grandma and Mama weren't yelling at each other now that they were back.

"Do you know how much we missed you, sweetie?"

"Don't be sad, Grandma. We came back to see you."

"Ginny, can you tell me what happened? Why you had to leave?"

"Mama said I wasn't supposed to say anything."

"I don't want you to tell me anything you don't want to, Ginny. But it might help you feel better. And I promise I won't let on to your mama."

So Ginny told her grandmother about the night before they left, when Dwayne had gone out with his friends and come home late and drunk. How he'd crashed through the door and started yelling and knocking things over and woke Ginny and Mama up. How he and Mama shouted at each other and Ginny watched out the window as Dwayne ran outside and tried to drive off in the van and was yelling at Mama to give him the keys and she wouldn't, so he picked up a wooden sawhorse and threw it at her. She jumped out of the way, but it hit her on the leg and made her fall down. And then Dwayne pried the keys out of Mama's hand and drove away and Ginny ran downstairs and helped her mother inside. Mama had put a bag of frozen hash browns on her leg and gave Ginny a Tylenol and put her back to bed, then woke her up a few hours later and helped her put her clothes and her teddies in garbage bags as quietly as they could.

"And then we took it all outside to the van and Dwayne was sleeping on the couch and we had to walk right by him without waking him up. And then we drove all day to come here."

"My poor little dolly. No matter what happens, I'm not going to let you get hurt any more."

"But I didn't get hurt, Grandma. It was Mama who got the bruise on her leg."

Grandma sighed and shook her head. "I know you didn't, sweetheart, not like that. But you're still a little girl, and you need to be with people who can look after you and take care of you."

"But Mama takes care of me."

"And she'll keep taking care of you, baby. But what I mean is…I don't want you to move away ever again. Do you want to leave your grandma and grandpa again? Or do you want to stay near us?"

"I want us to stay here. Virginia was okay, but I missed my friends and I missed you and Grandpa and Sunday school and our old house."

"Well, then, that's settled. No more going away from each other, right?" Grandma smiled and patted Ginny's hand and then the kettle whistled and she made hot chocolate with marshmallows on top for both of them and told Ginny about how to make stuffing.

❋   ❋   ❋

Joe and Debby returned from the store and Ginny ran out to help them with the bags. She loved Grandma's Thanksgiving dinner: turkey and stuffing and biscuits and gravy and sweet potato casserole with browned marshmallows on top. She could hardly wait for Thursday, just the four of them, eating a big dinner together that Ginny helped to make. She hoped one day to be as good a cook as Grandma.

After the groceries were put away, Ginny shucked corn for that night's dinner while Debby smoked in the rocking chair and read a *People* magazine. Some cars pulled into the lot next door: a red pickup and a silver SUV. The cabin had been rented to lots of different people over the years. Ginny remembered the time the boy with the curly blonde hair had been staying there. He looked like a cherub off a valentine and Ginny had chased him around all weekend playing kissing tag. But these people were all grownups, men with beards and ladies in tight jeans. Mama sat up straighter in her seat and pulled her sweater around her neck. "Hey, I think I know that guy...is that Ed?" She stood up and squinted. "Ed?" she said in a sort of half-yell.

The man with the biggest beard looked over. He squinted too. "Debby Dunn—is that you?"

"Oh my god, I don't believe it!" Her mother squealed like she only did around boys, and jumped off the porch. Ed bounded across the yard and picked Ginny's mother up like a sack of potatoes, while she kicked her legs and screamed. He put her down and they hugged.

"What are you doing up here?" Debby asked.

"Oh, just came up for some hunting with a few friends. I remembered when we booked the place that your folks had a place up here somewheres, but I didn't think I'd be right beside it."

"What are the odds, huh?"

"So, your folks are still keeping this place up?"

Debby nodded. "Still driving me nuts too."

"Well, what have you been up to all these years?" he asked.

"Oh, honey, that's an awful long story."

"Well, listen, why don't you come over tonight for a few beers, tell me all about the last ten years or so?"

"Man, I would love to."

"All right then. C'mon over after supper and we'll tip a few." He wandered back over to his cabin, where a cooler was already set up on the porch.

"Who was that?" Ginny asked.

"Oh, just an old friend from high school," said Debby. She looked at Ginny as if just remembering that she was there. "Sorry I didn't introduce you, baby."

"It's okay."

"I will next time, yeah? Here—you wanna read my magazine? I'm going to take a shower."

❉   ❉   ❉

That night, Ginny couldn't sleep. The back bedroom was cold and the little wrought-iron bed felt strange without her mother in it to cuddle her and keep her warm. She could hear country music coming from the cabin next door and wondered when Mama would be home.

When Mama was getting ready to leave after supper, Grandma had told her that the last thing she needed was to get mixed up with another bum. Mama had told her to mind her own business and that it was wrong to judge people Grandma hadn't even heard tell of in ten years. Grandpa had taken Ginny by the shoulder and steered her out to the porch, where they had played a few rounds of Go Fish and tried to ignore the shouting and the slamming door.

Ginny crept out of bed and opened the garbage bag with her teddy bears in it. She pulled out Mr. Oatmeal and Floppy Dog and set them on the bed. Then she dug to the bottom of the bag and felt around for the compact rectangle that was her deck of cards. She climbed back into bed and slid the cards under the pillow, but kept her hand curled tightly around them. She thought about how she would surprise her mother by being awake when she came home, and she lay on her side and looked at her teddies and tried not to close her eyes, but she did close them just for a minute and when she opened them again, it was light in the room and she heard the coffee percolator going and Grandma scuffing around in her slippers, and Ginny was still alone in the bed.

In the kitchen, Grandpa sat at the table with a plate of fried eggs. Mama sat beside him, picking at a piece of toast and wearing the same clothes she'd had on yesterday.

"Good morning, sweetheart," said Grandma. "Are you ready for some breakfast?"

Ginny nodded and her mother regarded her with a bleary kindness. "Hey, baby," she rasped. "Did you have a good sleep?"

"She got more than you did, I'm sure," said Grandma, cracking an egg into the sizzling pan.

Debby scrunched her face behind her mother's back and patted the chair beside her. "The guys next door have all gone hunting today," she told Ginny.

"Maybe you'll be able to spend some time with your little girl, then," said Grandma.

She saw Grandpa give her a funny look.

"Course we will," said Debby, patting Ginny's hand. "Maybe we can go for a walk later or something."

After breakfast, Mama sat in front of the TV and plucked her eyebrows and watched makeover shows and fell asleep.

※　※　※

Ginny was peeling a turnip on the front porch for Grandma late that afternoon when Ed's truck roared into the yard. The men piled out in their hunting gear, high-fiving each other and talking in loud excited voices. Ed went around to the back, opened the tailgate and pulled a large doe to the edge of the truck bed headfirst. Her soft brown body was splayed across a camo-printed tarp. The men gathered closer, and Ginny could see through the spaces between their bodies to the doe's empty eyes, the line of blackened blood that ran down the side of her mouth, the dark slit in her belly where she'd been gutted in the field. Debby stepped out on the porch and walked over to Ed. Ginny could see that she had put on lipstick and brushed her hair.

"Doe's good eatin'," Ed said, slapping the deer's side. "Let's get 'er strung up and dressed." He saw Debby and put his arm around her. Mama stood on her tippytoes and kissed Ed's thick neck. "I'll string you up next!" he shouted. "C'mere, Debby Dunn Dallas, and give me some of that," he said, smacking her wide denim-clad backside. She leapt up and scampered away, giggling. Ed turned and saw Ginny standing on the porch. He waved at her. "Wanna come see your Thanksgiving dinner?" he said. "We're having Bambi!" He laughed and Mama punched his arm and Ginny picked up her turnip and went inside.

❄ ❄ ❄

Most of the deer meat would improve with aging, but the tougher cuts needed to be cooked the next day. Grandma had offered to make it into a stew alongside the Thanksgiving dinner, and Debby invited Ed to join them. The big silver stew pot bubbled away on the stove for most of the afternoon, filling the cabin with the smell of venison. Ginny made a point of covering her nose and mouth every time someone looked at her.

Ed and Debby had been drinking beer on the back porch since before lunch, half-talking, half-shouting. Ginny was setting the table when they finally came in, the screen door thwacking in the frame. Ed stood over the stove and breathed in the steam from the pot. He asked Ginny's mother about the seasoning: did it need more salt, could it use some pepper? Debby pulled up a chair beside Ginny and flashed her a wobbly grin. Her hair hung low over her red eyes.

"Goddamn!" Ed said. "That's hot!" He tossed the wooden spoon on the counter and fanned his mouth with his hands like a cartoon bear. He lumbered to the table and took a long pull from Ginny's can of orange soda.

As he swished it around in his mouth, he ruffled her hair with a heavy palm. He swallowed and belched.

"Looking forward to your supper tonight, I bet? Stew's gonna be the best dinner you ever had," he said, setting down the can.

Ginny looked at the soda with disgust. "It will not. That deer probably had little babies and you killed their mother and that's a sin."

"Ginny, don't talk to our guest like that," said her grandmother.

"It's all right, Missus Dunn. Ginny here just doesn't know much about deer," said Ed. His words were soft, but his face looked angry. "See, if we didn't kill some of them deer, they'd over-breed and then there wouldn't be enough food to go around and they'd starve. Besides, it's late enough in the season that any fawns left behind would make it on their own."

"That's right, sweetie," her mother slurred, as though she knew more about deer than Ginny.

Ginny dug her fingernails into the legs of her jeans to keep from crying.

At dinner, Ed pulled faces at Debby during grace (Ginny had opened her eyes a slit to watch them). He and Debby poured themselves plenty of wine from the white Gallo box, and Ed chewed with his mouth open and Debby didn't seem to notice.

Grandma tried to keep the conversation moving. "So, Ed," she asked, "what do you do for a living?"

"I was working at the John Deere plant until it shut down. Got a good severance package, but that's nearly gone. Now I'll have to find something else, I suppose."

Debby patted his shoulder. "Don't worry, baby, you will."

Ginny looked at the two of them, at how easily Debby had wrapped herself around Ed. It was like they had always been this way, like there had never been a Dwayne, or even a Daddy. Ginny wondered if Ed and Mama would be together now, if he'd move them to some other state and Ginny would have to make new friends again and sleep in a new room. She looked at her grandma and grandpa, who each smiled at her. Grandpa reached over and put another biscuit on her plate without her even having to ask. She wished she could crawl onto his lap right there and start sucking her thumb, like she used to when she was little.

"Gonna fill up on biscuits?" Ed asked, smiling. "What about this nice stew your granny made, aren't you going to have any?"

Ginny looked at the bowl with the chunks of meat floating in brown gravy. She shook her head. All she could think of was the deer's dead eyes.

❋ ❋ ❋

After dinner, Mama and Ed went for a drive. The kitchen had heated up the house so much that Ginny sat on the back porch without a jacket, half-heartedly playing a game of Solitaire. She kept looking over at the shed where the doe had been hung and dressed. She thought about the little deer babies that might have been left behind, until she got herself crying and hot-faced. Grandpa was watching a show about football, so Ginny snuck off the back porch and went around to the front of the house to go back inside. That way she could get to her bedroom and only see Grandma, and she didn't mind so much if Grandma saw her crying. As she came around the side of the house, Ed's truck pulled in. Ginny stopped and flattened herself into the corner made by the chimney. Ed cut the lights, but neither he nor Mama got out. Ginny could see the flame of a lighter lighting their faces, and then a small orange ember moving between the two of them. As her eyes adjusted to the darkness, she could make out their faces through the windshield. Mama's face looked sad. Ed leaned in and said something to Mama, and Ginny couldn't tell if it was something funny or sad, but Mama's neck stretched back and her teeth showed. Then Ed kissed Mama's neck, and then his face moved down her chest. He seemed to be holding on to her hair. When he let go, Mama's head slumped forward like a doll's, and she wiped her nose on the back of her wrist. Ginny could see only the top part of Ed's head. His baseball cap was on backwards.

Ginny yelped out an Indian yell and ran in front of the truck. Both their faces popped up in the windshield as she passed them, and she kept whooping as she ran in her sock feet across the road and into the forest. Once she'd passed the first few trees, the darkness and the silence of the forest enveloped her. Ginny knew she was acting like a baby, but didn't stop running. She knew her Daddy would be angry with her if he were here, and she wished he was. She zigzagged through the trees even as she could hear voices yelling her name in the distance. She ran until she was sweating and her mouth tasted like she'd been sucking pennies. When Ginny turned around, she couldn't hear anyone, and she couldn't see any houses or lights. The forest was a curtain that had closed up behind her with rows of trees everywhere she turned.

Ginny sat down against one of the trees, onto the soft bed of needles at its base. She wished she had Mr. Oatmeal with her, or Floppy Dog, or even her deck of cards, even though it was too dark to see much of anything. Ginny stuck her thumb in her mouth and closed her eyes. The cold prickled under her shirt. She prayed to Jesus, her lips moving around her small thumb. She asked him to bring the deer to her to lead her out of the forest. Ginny imagined their arrival, heeding the call, deer by the dozens, whitetails by the hundreds, all coming for her and her recognizing every one, a stampede of firm and dainty legs whistling through the tall dark trees.

I SET MY ALARM AND GET OUT OF THE HOUSE EARLY SO I CAN buy the test at the drug store. That alone is probably going to make everyone suspicious, like what I am doing out of bed before noon on a Saturday? Before I leave, I check one more time to see if my period has come. It's the only time in my life that I've actually wished for cramps, backache, anything. I'm almost two weeks late.

The last few days have been so emo. I go back and forth between worrying and half-praying (even though I'm like the least Christian person ever) and then being really optimistic like everything's going to be fine. The worst part has been not telling anyone. At first, I thought I'd tell Jade, but that's like announcing it on Facebook. Of course, I should be telling Brandon, but I haven't figured out how. I've thought about it, but I don't have any actual information to give him. What am I supposed to say? I might

Tested

be? I could be? I can almost see his head tipping in that cute sideways way it does, and him looking like he just doesn't get it. He'll want some kind of answer. And I won't have one. Well, not yet anyway.

The tests are way more expensive than I thought they'd be, like the first time I had to buy my own tampons. Nearly all the tests come in packs of two. It seems like it's just a way to rip people off, but then I figure it must be so you can do it twice in case you don't believe it the first time. Really, they should make them in triple-packs, so you could do the best two out of three. In commercials, the ladies who use these things are always married and totally wanting to have a baby. They never show anyone sketchy or in high school, but I bet that's who buys most of them. The people who are hoping they're not.

Of course I have to see a pregnant lady in the lineup at the cash. She's so big and round, she's like a parade float. I keep looking around to see if there's anyone I know in the store. It would be a bad time to run into someone's mom. Now I wish I had told someone, so I'd have someone to stand beside me. I feel like a juvenile delinquent, one who doesn't even have friends.

I go next door to the Tim Hortons and head upstairs to the ladies' room. There's no way I'm going to take this thing home with me and then have to hide the evidence. I'd rather do it here and get it over with. There's no one else in the bathroom, thank god, and I get in the stall and get out the instruction booklet. It says for the best and most accurate results, you should do the test with "your first morning urine," which means I've already screwed it up. But it claims it should still work, and I've come this far. The rest of the directions are pretty easy—just pee on the stupid thing. The hardest part is getting the stick out of the plastic wrapper. I have to tear it with my teeth, then I worry that a spit molecule has gotten into the test and ruined it. I squat and hold the stick into the pee stream. I'm so nervous I get a bit of pee on my hand. Gross. I put the cap on and set it down on top of the toilet paper dispenser after I put a few sheets of toilet paper on it to make a clean spot. You're not supposed to shake the test around or blow on it or anything, just leave it alone for three minutes. I get out my iPhone and set the timer. This might be the longest three minutes of my life.

0:12
What if it's positive? Who will I tell? What will I do? There's no way I'm telling my parents. My mom would freak. She had like, three miscarriages before me, and she always talks about how she wanted to get pregnant so bad. And then after me, everything went weird and she wasn't able to have any more kids, so I guess I'm the miracle baby. If I am knocked up, she'd probably be one of those creepy moms who makes her kid keep going to school and raises the baby as her own and then I have to spend the rest of my life acting like my kid is really just my little brother or

sister. That's random, like a Lifetime Network movie. It might make her feel really sad, actually, after she had to work so hard to have a baby and being in the hospital all those times, for me to get this way so easily, just by accident. If I was her, I'd be pissed off. It's totally not fair that some people who want to get pregnant have such a hard time and then the ones who don't want to or don't mean to just do without even trying.

1:04

I'm such a dumbass, I don't even have a good excuse. Brandon's the only guy I've ever done it with and even that's only been a few times. Every other time we used a condom and then we got this unexpected opportunity, let's just say, and we didn't have one and went for it anyway. He pulled out, but obviously not in time. I've been meaning to go on the Pill. There's a Planned Parenthood clinic nearby and everything, but I just hadn't gotten around to it yet. I guess, no, I promise, that if the test is negative, I'll go there right away and walk in and get on the Pill. If.

1:27

If it's positive, I'll have to tell some people. And I guess I'll have to find out about getting an abortion. We went by this place in Jade's mom's car one day, and there were these people standing on the side of the road and yelling and waving big signs with pictures on them and at first I didn't know what the pictures were, because they just looked like a big blobby mess. And then I read the words and figured it out. I read one sign out loud by mistake. Abortion Kills Babies. Jade said, "Yeah, isn't that the point?" and I laughed, but her mom got really mad at her. But really, isn't that the point? Like, whether or not you think that's a good thing, that's kind of what it does. And even if you don't believe in it, it's gotta be better than waiting until after the kid's born. I saw on the news last week that the cops found somebody's baby in a plastic bag in a landfill. That's so shitty, throwing your baby in the garbage. I promise that no matter what happens, I won't do that. I won't be one of those trashy girls in the States that you read about who has her baby in the toilet at prom and leaves it to die while she goes back to dancing.

2:16
But here I am, in a toilet stall already, doing my pregnancy test, so I'm probably not any better than anyone else. I don't want to have a kid. I'm not ready. Moms are supposed to have their lives together, are supposed to know what they're doing. I hate when you're at the mall or wherever and you see a super-young mom and she's all tired and bitchy and yelling at her kid. Sometimes they grab the kid too roughly, or just talk to them like they're stupid and they hate them. That's so mean. It's not your kid's fault that you're not cut out for this job. But now I see that I could be that mom. Putting Coke in the kid's bottle and other stupid shit.

2:39
I looked up on Wikipedia about pregnancy tests. They used to have to do it at the doctor's office and then they'd inject a rabbit with your pee and then they'd kill it after three days and look at its ovaries and that's how they could tell. I'm glad I don't have to kill any rabbits and I'm glad I don't have to wait three days. Please god, please please let everything be okay.

3:03
In the window, there's a little minus sign. I reread the instructions and make sure that means what I think it means. I instantly understand why they give you two tests in a box, since I get the second one out right away to make sure. I didn't think to save any pee for this one, so I have to think about running a bath, dipping my hand in warm water. I can only squeeze out a shotglass worth, but it's enough. This time I stand over the test and watch the little window until the minus sign shows up again, and then I put both tests in the silver garbage can. The box falls into the corner, but it's gross back there, so I just leave it.

I leave the stall, wash my hands and put on some lip gloss. I'm happy that it's good news and everything, and I feel totally relieved, but…it's like I've just run up a bunch of stairs, or a big balloon has just burst. I think I might cry, but then I decide that it's probably nothing an iced cappuccino and a maple-dip donut can't fix. I'd text Jade or Brandon or anyone, but I just want to be quiet and alone for a little while longer. Everyone's still sleeping anyway.

Blink.
Blink.
Blink.

EMILY STARED OUT THE WINDOW ABOVE THE TELEVISION SET.
A string of lights on the neighbours' back porch flashed white / off /
white / off. She tried to time her blinks, first so that all she saw was
white, then all she saw was off. Christmas Eve shows were shit anyway;
three of their five channels showing *It's a Wonderful Life*. Their Christ-
mas tree, all six inches of it, sat lopsided atop the set, with its flocked wire branches and little red beads meant to look like ornaments. It came in the mail with the other family gifts, long since opened and discarded or pressed into use: socks, chocolates, a Santa mug whose handle broke off in the box.

Communion

Emily pressed play on the CD player again and watched Carrie roll a
joint on the coffee table. Occasionally something in the movie happened
in time to the music, and Carrie laughed as the black-and-white couples
danced and jumped into the swimming pool to The Red Hot Chili Peppers.
Carrie turned it up, and the gay guy upstairs counterattacked with Erasure.
Emily decided to run a bath. When she turned the taps, the pipes banged
and shrieked as though the water was being beaten out of them.

"At least there's weed," said Emily, lifting a hand out of the bath water as Carrie passed the joint. Carrie perched on the toilet, knees up and
long purple toenails curled around the lip of the tub.

"And Bailey's, too," Carrie chirped. "It's just not Christmas without it."

"Yeah." Emily was unconvinced. The squat brown bottle had cost almost as much as a week's supply of shitty beer. They'd spent most of the December welfare cheque already. In six days, the rent would be due and the Bailey's would be long gone.

"What do you want to do tomorrow?" Carrie asked.

What Emily wanted to do was crawl into bed and stay there. "We could go downtown and walk around," she offered.

"Nobody will be there. Everything will be closed."

"Exactly."

Emily slid down until her head went under. She held her breath for as long as she could, feeling her hair float around her face. When she came up again, Carrie was gone.

The girls sat in front of the TV and ate the remaining chocolates in the Pot of Gold box, then pulled the coffee table aside to unfold the sofa bed. Emily had a futon in the bedroom, but their damp basement apartment had turned the mattress black with mildew.

She crawled in beside Carrie; it was warmer together, even if Carrie was a restless and talkative sleeper. Emily listened to the sounds outside, remembering how hard it had been as a kid to sleep on Christmas Eve. The rain running through the gutters didn't sound like the promise of snow.

✳   ✳   ✳

Emily awoke to Carrie sitting on the edge of the sofa bed, humming "Jingle Bells" and holding a mug out in front of her. "Merry Christmas, Emmy. I made a special coffee for a special Christmas girl."

"Thanks." Emily sat up and held the hot mug under her nose. The coffee, laced with Bailey's, smelled comforting.

"Still want to go downtown later?" Carrie asked.

Emily tried to be cheerful. "Sure thing. We could just ride around; see what's going on."

"It's even stopped raining."

"You know what we should do? Go downtown, but let's do the rest of those mushrooms first."

Carrie leapt up so quickly that Emily sloshed coffee on her T-shirt. "I'll put the kettle on for tea!"

Emily peeled the wet shirt from her chest, sucked the sweet booze out.

※　※　※

Emily and Carrie had become friends over mushrooms. They'd eaten some bad ones on an end-of-high school camping trip with classmates. They hung their heads out of their neighbouring tents all night, barfing and groaning, muttering words of sympathy and compassion to one another under the cold, starless sky.

Since then, tea was the only way either would take them. They turned the radio on and filled the teapot with mushrooms and Red Zinger tea bags and honey. Every so often, one of them would add boiling water and stir the sludge with a wooden spoon. They sat in bed together, drinking tea and listening to carols.

"I had a dream about Jason last night," Carrie said. Jason was the latest victim of one of Carrie's epic crushes. She had met him only a few times, but already he was her reason for living. Carrie had the power to spin a gossamer thread of attraction into something much more substantial using nothing more than her own imagination, and almost always, the object of her affection was willing to follow the fantasy she'd dreamt up. But so far, Jason had remained more interested in his bike and his bong than in Carrie, which gave Emily a secret thrill, and not just because she had liked him first. It was tiring to watch boys fall for Carrie, then get scared off by her drama. It was like one of those TV fishing shows, where the hosts reeled in fish after fish, only to have them thrash around in their hands until they finally let them back in the water. Emily was usually the one left stroking Carrie's head while she bawled her "what's wrong with me?" routine. But she never really expected an answer, and no one, least of all Emily, had the guts to tell her she just wanted too much from people, too soon, all of the time. And then it just started all over again anyway, with a boy from a record store, a guy at a coffee shop, somebody's boyfriend, a Thursday night DJ.

✳   ✳   ✳

Emily had known only one person in Victoria when she arrived three months ago: Crystal, who'd moved there to get her Engineering Degree at UVic and was too busy to spend much time with Emily. Then, walking downtown one day, she ran into Jason, who'd gone to her high school for a couple years until he moved away. Now he was living with a group of guys in a falling-down rental house near the Bay Street Bridge that Emily had christened Guyland. She had stopped by with beers a few times, and shared them with whatever assortment of boys was there. There was always a new assortment of skateboarders, rock climbers, and mountain bikers, each one more grimy and gorgeous than the last. Emily liked being the only girl at the endless party, hanging out among the empty beer cases and tools and camping equipment and overflowing ashtrays and bongs, at least until Carrie came along.

One night, Emily and Jason made out behind the couch where he had stationed his Thermarest and sleeping bag, while the party raged on around them. Then they went for a walk and smoked a joint together, and talked about music, and Emily had pretended to know things about bands, and then she had dragged him into some bushes near the park and laid down on the ground with him. They made out some more and she put her hand down his pants and started to undo her jeans. He sat up, looking around and pushing her away. "I…I can't do this here," he said.

"Why not?"

"Because it's cold and we're in some bushes in a park."

"It's still more private than your so-called bedroom." She rubbed her palm against his hard-on. "Don't you like me?"

"Of course I like you. I think you're...really cool. Let's just go back, okay?"

"So you're not going to fuck me."

"No."

"Why not?" Emily realized she was whining, but the seam of her jeans pressed against her crotch and intensified the need for something inside her.

"Because you deserve better than this."

This made her laugh. "No I don't," she said.

※ ※ ※

Emily thought about Jason and the Guyland boys while Carrie talked, and then wondered what time it was. And what time would it be back in Ontario? After lunch, for sure. All the presents would be open, and the turkey was probably in the oven already. Emily's family would be eating cheese and crackers and chocolates in front of the fire, and maybe waiting for her to call...

And then the visuals kicked in. Red graph paper drifted in front of her eyes and Carrie's ramblings started to sound more interesting. After all, who was Emily to say that Carrie's dreams of love weren't legitimate messages from the Great Beyond? And then everything became slumber-party funny and Emily rolled around on the bed and laughed until she almost peed herself because Carrie kept pressing her teaspoon over Emily's eye and pretending to be an optometrist.

"I think," said Carrie, smacking the spoon on the sheets, "that if we're going to go out on Christmas Day, we should look the part. Like elves or something!"

"But what do we have that's Christmassy?"

"You know, anything that has like, red or green on it, or bells or sparkles."

"In that case, I'll just have a browse in the 'gay apparel' section of our wardrobe, shall I?" which sent them both into mushroom hysterics again.

Emily went through the closet and the laundry basket, pulling out anything red or green, which wasn't much. Carrie pawed through drawers, pulling out an emerald-coloured crushed-velvet bodysuit. She paired it with her usual black fishnets under jean cut-offs and black boots, while Emily found a dark green babydoll dress with little pink flowers on it (that looked kind of red if you squinted), black tights, and her old red Converse high-tops.

Emily finished dressing and listened while Carrie phoned her parents. After a few bursts of Portuguese-peppered English, Carrie started crying. Not surprising, since Carrie's parents were total assholes. With her three older sisters married and cranking out grandkids, it was obvious that they were done with this final daughter, their family's loudest, skankiest disappointment. But it never stopped Carrie from talking about her parents like they were saints.

"Oh, Daddy, I miss you so much! How are you? Do you miss me too? What did you say? No, no, I know, I can hear all the kids…they must be so happy. *I love you, Pai*! What? Okay, no, it's fine…can you put Mom back on for a second then?"

Carrie eventually hung up and smiled her best fake smile through her sniffles. "I probably shouldn'ta done that."

"I think you're right. C'mon, we need more festive attire, and I'm too high to deal with it alone," Emily said, waving a red scarf at her.

Carrie blew her nose and resumed the search, unearthing from beneath the dresser a pair of red-and-black striped tights with holes in the toes. She cut the legs off the tights, then cut each leg in half, so they could each have a pair of arm-warmers to wear over their tops. Emily pulled them on and discovered the thigh end was larger than the calf end. Carrie helped safety pin it to her sleeve to keep it from falling down, while they both laughed and sang "Deck the Halls." Emily fished a couple of discarded bows from their parents' presents out of the garbage and bobby pinned them into their hair. She and Carrie looked in the bathroom mirror together, taking turns standing on top of the toilet to see their whole outfits. They looked like poor, slutty versions of the girls who worked at Santa's workshop in the mall.

"We're so Christmassy," said Carrie.

"We're Christmassy as fuck," Emily agreed.

The phone rang and Emily grabbed it, hoping it was Carrie's dickface father. "Merry Whatever," she growled.

It was Emily's mother. "Hi Mommmmm," she squeaked. "What? No, I'm fine... Yeah, Merry Christmas to you too. What're you guys doing? Yeah, I guess so...hmmm. No, it's shitty here—sorry, Mom. What? No...well, Carrie bought some Bailey's so we've had some of that. Hey, Mom, do I sound really weird? Because I feel pretty fucking weird right now... Oh, sorry, Mom. Grandma's there already? Um, of course I want to talk to her, but here's the thing, Mom, I'm kinda fucked up right now, because..."

Carrie began flapping her hands around in Emily's face and silently screaming *NOOOOOO*.

"Because, um...I'm just really sad and I miss you guys. Can I call you back a little later? Uh-huh. Okay, love you too." Emily hung up and turned to Carrie. "If that phone rings again, I'm dead or not here or something."

"Dude, you just about blew your entire family's mind for Christmas. Neither of us is using that fucking phone again."

"Not even if Jason calls and wants to give you his Yule log?"

"Okay, maybe then. Hey, did you know it's been, like, three hours since we started getting ready?"

"Whoa—major mushroom time warp."

They both put their jackets on, and then some red lipstick.

❄   ❄   ❄

Emily's legs seemed to have forgotten how to ride a bike. Ahead, Carrie was wobbling too, her hair bow flapping around in the wind. Maybe they were going too fast, or too slow. Maybe people were looking at them through their living room windows and laughing. They headed downhill towards the water and stopped for a smoke when they got to the parking lot. There were a surprising number of people walking around, mostly men and kids, probably keeping out of the way while mothers set tables and basted turkeys. This was Emily's favourite spot in the city. She liked to sit on the rocks and watch people flying their kites in the park. There were no kites today, but Emily still saw them out of the corner of her eye, jumping blobs of purple and orange and red. They smoked in silence for a few minutes, listening to the water and the wind, the cars driving by.

❋   ❋   ❋

Emily had been eating a cup of instant noodles in front of the TV when someone knocked on her door. She'd opened it to Carrie, standing in the dark and the rain with a backpack and a suitcase at her feet and a small stuffed bear in her hands, which she thrust at Emily while screaming, "SURPRISE!" And yes, Emily had been surprised—and glad to see that familiar face. She had welcomed Carrie inside and made tea and they had hugged and talked and it wasn't until fifteen or twenty minutes had passed that Emily began to understand that her friend hadn't just come for a visit. She had moved in.

"Did you have anything to do with this?" She had phoned Steve the next day when Carrie was in the shower.

"Oh, I knew," he said. "I tried everything to get her to tell you, but you know how she is about surprises."

"Yeah, I got that. But why didn't you tell me anyway? I could have faked it."

"She said she'd be able to tell on your face if you were just pretending. She would have killed me."

"There was no danger of me not being surprised," said Emily, remembering how Carrie's scream had made her drop her noodles on the carpet.

She sighed. "And why is protecting Carrie's feelings the most important thing here?"

He lit a cigarette in the pause. "Look, I know, and I'm sorry—about the other thing too. But Carrie's still your friend, right? Aren't you still glad to see her?"

"Maybe." She flinched inside at the thought of the other thing. "But, dude, the next time I leave town," she said, trying to sound bored and worldly, "remind me not to give you an address."

"Did you just call me dude? What are you, a surfer now?"

✳ ✳ ✳

"Is it just me, or does everyone look a bit like Eugene Levy from a distance?" said Carrie, handing Emily her lighter. Emily wished Carrie could understand the concept of a comfortable silence.

"What about up close?"

"No, then they just look like themselves."

"You need glasses so bad."

"There's no way I'm wearing glasses—contacts maybe, but not glasses."

Emily pushed her own glasses up the bridge of her nose. She couldn't be bothered to put in her contacts when she was high. Carrie wouldn't do or wear anything that might make one less guy in the world be one iota less attracted to her. She had to have everyone hot for her or she felt like a hideous failure. Emily couldn't figure it out; Carrie was pretty, for sure, but there was no shortage of pretty girls. There was just something about her that made guys go crazy. Maybe they could sense how badly she needed them. Whenever they walked downtown, guys always said dirty things to Carrie, from young cute ones to gross old perverts, and she never flinched or said anything back; Emily was always the one who told them to go fuck themselves. Carrie just kept walking, half-smiling, like taking that shit was just part of the job of being her, like if it ever went away she would stop existing.

They finished their smokes and rode to the video store, but it was closed. They stood shivering and bored in the doorway.

Carrie pouted. "I'm hungry," she said.

"You're never hungry." Carrie lived on Diet Coke and cigarettes, and the occasional binge of a jumbo bag of chips and two or three chocolate bars in a sitting. Emily tried to eat like a normal person, but it wasn't easy. There was rarely any food in the house, and besides, Carrie calculated every morsel, Emily's included, in terms of how many sit-ups would be required to burn it off. Emily's softly rounded stomach was a constant source of irritation for Carrie, who cautioned her to do something before it "got worse."

"I don't think I'm hungry. I just feel high…and really fucking cold," said Emily.

"I bet Denny's is open—it's always open," Carrie suggested.

"That could be the most depressing dining experience ever."

"Or the most awesome."

Emily shrugged and got back on her bike. She hoped the drugs would provide some artificial enthusiasm on the way there.

The Denny's was almost empty in the sad stretch between lunch and dinner. The waitress had a face like a pit bull and seated them as though insulted by their very presence. They both ordered a Moons Over My Hammy and Carrie ordered a Diet Coke; Emily, tea. The menu was so colourful and shiny that when the waitress tried to take it away, Emily asked to keep it.

Carrie asked, "Oooh, do you guys have any crayons? And those placemats you can colour on?" The waitress looked even more disgusted and pivoted away. The next time she passed with the coffee pot, she dropped a foam cup of broken colours and a stack of placemats on their table.

"Thank you!" Carrie sang to her back. Then she started singing along to the tinny piped-in Christmas carols. Emily slid down in the booth, embarrassed even in front of the Denny's losers. Anytime, anywhere,

Carrie always sang along to whatever was playing: in restaurants, in taxis, at the mall…she had a good-enough voice, but she was no Aretha Franklin, yet here she was, belting out "Santa Claus is Coming to Town" like she was at Carnegie Hall.

Emily returned to the menu and its colourful depictions. She waited for Carrie to draw a breath and said, "Moons Over My Hammy makes me wish I could go somewhere hot right now; just lie on a real beach in the sun."

Carrie stopped mid-chorus. "How come?"

"How come I want to lie on a beach?"

"No, how come Moons Over My Hammy makes you think of a beach?"

"Um, My-'ammy?" No recognition. "Mi-ami? Moons over Miami?"

"Oh, it rhymes!" Carrie seemed delighted. "I never thought of that before."

Emily considered explaining further, but before she could, Carrie's face took on its serious cloudy look. "If I could go anywhere, know where I'd go?" she asked.

"Where?"

"I'd go home," she said and, like a well-trained movie star, her dark-lined eyes instantly brimmed with tears.

"Oh, for fuck's sake," Emily said, setting down the menu. "Don't cry. Don't do this, Carrie, you'll make yourself crazy."

"I know, but I just miss my family soooo much. It was one thing when they were only an hour away, but now they're so far and I can't just see them whenever I want to!"

"Yeah, I know…but you're always obsessed with whatever you can't have."

"I'm what?"

"Nothing," Emily said. "Forget it. I'm just coming down a bit and getting bummed out. Let's just eat our food and get out of here, go smoke a joint."

"No—what do you mean; I'm obsessed with what I can't have?"

Emily sighed. "I just mean that, like, with your parents, or guys, or whatever, that you get really interested in something or someone if you can't get it. Like, if a guy already has a girlfriend or lives out of town or whatever. That's all I meant, but, like, everyone does that, right? We all do that."

"Well, Merry fucking Christmas." Carrie picked up a crayon and, head down, began filling in the placemat maze.

"Aw, come on...I'm really sorry, okay? I didn't mean anything. I don't want you to be sad, that's all. Your parents aren't even—"

Her head popped up. "Oh, now what, you're gonna talk shit about my parents too?" She was dangerously near to shouting.

"I was going to say that they're not even here, so there's no point in worrying about them," Emily said with finality, but Carrie didn't look fooled.

The waitress arrived with their plates and plunked them down at the table's edge. Emily slid the ketchup over to Carrie. "C'mon," she said. "It's Christmas, right? Let's not fight." But even as she said it, there was an urge inside her to have that fight, to tell her to go fuck herself, with her sulking and her stupid surprises and her boyfriend stealing and her bullshit. Emily imagined tipping Carrie's plate into her lap, dumping the glass of Diet Coke over her head. Instead, she pulled the container of sugar over. Every restaurant in town had the Commonwealth Games sugar packets with the cartoon killer-whale mascot in various sporting events. Carrie's favourite was the skeet-shooting one, because it featured the manically grinning orca standing on his tail fin and clutching a rifle. Emily found one in the container and set it beside Carrie's plate. "See? I even got you a Christmas present and everything."

"That reminds me..." Carrie said, rummaging through her mini backpack. She pulled out a small red box with a white ribbon tied around it.

"What's this?"

"It's your present," she said. "Open it," she added without enthusiasm. Carrie usually loved giving presents.

Inside the box was a pair of earrings: silver hoops with a swirly rainbow bead. Emily had seen them at a stall in Market Square weeks before but couldn't afford them. "Carrie, oh my god..."

"They weren't that expensive," she grumbled.

Emily remembered agreeing that they wouldn't buy each other gifts; that their gifts to each other would be the booze and weed that they went halfers on. She twisted inside with guilt as she watched Carrie finger the sugar packet, and for a moment Emily wondered if maybe that was the point. She smiled her most grateful, kindest smile. "I'm going to the bathroom to put them on. Come with me?"

"Nah, you go ahead."

Emily didn't look good. Being high and staring at her own face was always a bad idea. The bluish anti-heroin light of the restroom wasn't helping, casting shadows under her eyes and making her skin look sallow. She put the earrings on and turned her head back and forth, the little beads sliding around. They were lovely. She'd have to try and save some money in the next few weeks to get Carrie a present too. Maybe a new journal. Carrie loved to write poetry and read it to Emily. Emily never knew what to say. Honestly, she thought it was pretty bad, but she could never say that. Any response weaker than unbridled enthusiasm could send Carrie into a daylong funk. Emily wrote in a diary sometimes too, but having to share its contents with anyone was her worst nightmare. She didn't want to know what other people thought about it, least of all Carrie. When she'd arrived, one of the first things Emily did was to slide her small coil-bound notebook above one of the suspended tiles in the basement ceiling.

❋ ❋ ❋

When Emily first arrived in Victoria and phoned her parents, her mother told her Steve had been calling. She managed to hold out for three full days before she called him back.

"Where the hell have you been?"

"I'm fine thanks, how are you?"

"Spare me. Did your mother give you the messages?"

"Yeah."

"I almost drove to the airport to stop you, you know."

"Why didn't you?" Emily imagined a movie scene, joyful tears and running down carpeted corridors.

"I don't know. I guess I was worried about what would happen next. I miss you."

"Maybe you should have thought of that before you dumped me."

"I didn't dump you—stop fucking saying that! I just got freaked out. Maybe if you'd given me a chance instead of jumping on a plane, we could have talked about it."

Emily sighed. Every conversation she had with Steve now made her feel queasy. "I got tired of talking. I wanted to do something for once."

There was a silence. She could hear a siren on the other end of the line. "Listen, I have to tell you about something that happened."

She could always tell when Steve was going to give her bad news; his voice dropped lower, just like it got higher when he was angry.

"Carrie and I, we, um, kind of...got together on the night you left."

Emily hadn't known this, but hearing it, it made perfect sense. Steve had surely wanted to punish Emily by screwing someone. And who better to do it with than one of her own friends? As far as loyalty, Carrie had none when it came to guys. She'd always been hot for Steve anyway, sticking her boobs in his face all the time. Emily bit the skin around her nails. "So?"

"So? Is that all you're going to say? Okay, so, it was just a one-time thing. I was hammered and fucking depressed and it just happened and I wanted to tell you before you found out from someone else."

"Really. Like who?"

"I dunno, I just didn't want one of your friends to tell you."

Emily laughed. "It's okay, Steve. I don't have friends anymore. I had to move thousands of miles to get away from all my so-called friends. But guess what? It turns out that you and your stupid shit can transcend time and space."

"Don't say that. I said I was sorry."

No, you didn't, thought Emily. "Why should I care, anyway? We were already broken up."

"Just—look. Don't say anything to Carrie, okay? You know what she's like. She made me promise not to tell you and she was really upset about it after."

"Yeah, I know what she's like." Emily snorted. "I bet she was really hurting. I bet you two had a good cry about it. Right after you fucked."

Silence. She imagined Steve smoking in his ugly brown chair in the corner of the apartment, with his legs tucked under him like some skinny kid.

"It wasn't like that. It was…let's just forget it, okay? Please? I miss you, Em. I really miss you."

She wouldn't give him the satisfaction of saying it back.

❋   ❋   ❋

Emily looked at the girl in the Denny's bathroom mirror. She'd moved across the country to change her life, and everything was still exactly the same. The same people, the same shit, the same Emily never saying what she really thought or felt about anything. What a joke. If she'd known nothing would get better, if she'd known she'd still be lonely and confused about everything, if she'd known she'd still be saddled with a best friend she wanted to choke half the time, she could have just stayed home. Now she was stuck here, because the only thing worse than staying would be to give up and go crawling back home. "God, you're a stupid bitch," she said. The girl made a face and shook her new earrings to and fro.

❋ ❋ ❋

On the ride home, Carrie slowed down and stopped in front of the big Catholic church. The doors were open and people in suits and dresses were filing inside. Carrie got off her bike and walked it over to the bike rack.

"What are you doing?"

"I'm going to church," she said, taking her lock out of her backpack. "Just like I have every other year with my family," she said, giving Emily a wounded look.

"Um, aren't we a little weird-looking for church? Maybe? And a little high?" Emily felt a fist of panic clenching in her chest.

"Speak for yourself," Carrie said haughtily. "I'm fine."

"Okay, well…wouldn't you rather go to Guyland or something, see if anyone's there?"

Even the promise of boys wasn't going to work. "You go if you want. I'm going to church. Do what you like." Short sentences out of Carrie were always a bad sign.

"Well, I'm not letting you go in there alone," Emily said.

"Fine. Just try not to fuck anything up. Do what I do."

They stepped inside and Carrie dipped her fingers in the holy water and crossed herself. Emily did the same but couldn't remember the right order. Spectacles, testicles, wallet and watch—but what side was for watch and what side was for wallet?

They slid into the end of a crowded pew near the back. Carrie wouldn't even look at her. Emily picked up a hymnal and tried to predict the order of events. She'd dated a Catholic guy in grade ten, and had been inside a Catholic church a few times, but most of it was a mystery. When the Mass started, she tried to follow along with whatever everyone else was doing, feeling like a neon sign was flashing *SINNER* over her head. After a couple of hymns and prayers, people began filing towards the front for Communion. As Emily mentally composed a list of recent sins—lying to her parents, smoking, drinking, taking drugs, premarital sex, hating her friends, the occasional shoplifting, taking the Lord's name in vain—Carrie rose to her feet and tugged down the hem of her cut-offs with exaggerated dignity.

"What are you doing?" Emily whispered.

"I'm receiving Communion," Carrie hissed, staring straight ahead.

Emily hoisted herself up, level with Carrie's shoulder. "But...don't you have to confess first?" Emily remembered from her old high-school boyfriend that you couldn't take Communion without making regular confessions—because he'd avoided both during their four months of frantic, furtive sex.

Carrie finally looked at Emily and her mouth was a hard thin line. "I don't have any sins to confess." Then she turned and walked away.

Emily sat down. She could smell the sweet reek of Dewberry perfume left where Carrie had been sitting. She watched as her friend sashayed towards the altar in her fishnets and cutoffs and falling-down stripy arm warmers. Every face in the church followed her progression up the aisle. She held her head high, just as she had when she had walked into Emily's apartment with all her stuff, or when some guy on the street told her to suck his cock. The way she probably walked out of Steve's apartment the morning after she screwed him.

Emily was hot and cold and dizzy all at once, her guts turning to liquid. She clenched her teeth, lurched from the pew and made her way out the door. Outside, in the little strip of holly bushes beside the church, she dropped to her knees and threw up her Moons Over My Hammy and mushrooms and tea and Bailey's. It burned her throat and her nose. She wiped her mouth with an arm warmer and untangled her hair from the holly branches. She retched again, but nothing came out. Her insides felt pummeled and raw.

Emily turned away from her puke and sat on the pavement. She rubbed her muddy hands on her dress, and saw her tights were torn at the knee. She hoped no one would notice her. She thought about getting up and walking to her bike, but her legs were stiff and cold. She whispered, "Come on, just get your shit together, man." Her voice sounded pathetic. She started to shiver, and reached up to pull her hair off her clammy neck. In one ear, she felt the cool weight of one silver beaded hoop. In the other, there was nothing. From inside the church, the congregation began to sing.

BLONDE WAS ALWAYS TRYING TO LET THE WIND OUT OF HIS sails, take him down a peg or two in front of everyone in the store. She had little regard for his position, for his commitment to the customer service vision, for his stupid business diploma. Just a bag of hot air, she said, to anyone in earshot. The big blowhard was pushing for a job at head office, she said, climbing the corporate ladder on everyone's backs. Secretly, she stood close to him during their morning meetings to smell the nicotine on his skin, the smell of her father.

She accused him of cutting her hours, of shorting her cheques, of stealing her lunch. He raised his palms like a supplicant and asked if they could take their battles to the pool hall.

Blonde

Blonde laughed at him and went with him and hung her cleavage like a dare over the deep green felt. She never got good at the game, but when they played doubles, she created an amusing-enough distraction that was sometimes sufficient for them to win.

Theirs was an uneasy alliance, filled with defenses and imagined slights. He didn't want to be her boyfriend because it violated staff policy. Who'd want you for a boyfriend anyway? she asked, tongue out. But she found herself wishing for beauty that would render him defenseless. He could avoid her for an entire shift, then sneak up behind her at the time clock and squeeze her shoulders through her boxy polo shirt. Blonde would never admit that his indifference to her was the greatest aphrodisiac. She began smoking again, found herself borrowing from his crummy collection of old-man music. They sat for hours in his parked car outside her apartment and argued about romance. He kept his hands on the wheel, even then. He told her that his disease was the physical manifestation of an inability to love, but the way he watched her exhale, she thought he was just a good liar. She told him her disease was the physical manifestation of the world being a bad joke. Not sick, exactly, just not quite right. Her hair, impossibly glossy, rested nightly on a metal stand. The holy trinity of Blonde, Brunette, and Redhead completed on a row of styrofoam heads in the closet. You could tell a lot about a man by his colour preference, just like leg men were different from tit men. It didn't surprise her that Blonde was his favourite. She didn't like to talk about it, but she would have told him anything if it would break his self-imposed vows. Anything to be the one who had the power to ruin him.

One night at the pool hall, an enthusiastic drunk chick hugged Blonde off balance and she felt the wig slipping off her head in slo-mo, those perfect honeyed waves sliding down her back and at last to the floor, like a dressing gown in an old movie, or a defrocked superhero's discarded cape. Drunk herself, Blonde retrieved it like a fumbled football and ran outside. She hid behind a monster truck in the parking lot and plopped the disheveled mess back on her hairless head.

He found her and held her while she cried and helped her adjust her bangs. She wiped her nose on his shoulder, looked up at him and laughed through her tears when she saw the look of pity and kindness on his face. Let's go dancing, she said. She walked back through the bar to collect her jacket like nothing could touch her. Later, outside the night-club, he told her she was the bravest girl he'd ever met. Since she'd now played every card she had, since he'd now seen her more naked than naked, she stood on her toes and kissed him. At last, she thought, as they necked on the sidewalk, his erection pressing against her stomach, I'm the one in charge.

❋   ❋   ❋

Weeks later, she stood in the doorway of his bedroom, watching him sleep, and contemplated the contagion of his illness. His inability to love hadn't interfered during those first nights and days in bed fueled by sex and jazz cassettes on endless loops and smoking. But before the end of the first month, the booze-and-pills cocktails fueled more all-day naps than marathon fucks. He called in sick to the store for days running, pleading flu, and she just stopped showing up. He called her fat. She hated the face he made when he came. She forgot just what it was that had made her want to change him so badly. She never wanted to listen to a Leonard Cohen album again. The bedclothes stank. Whatever sickness he had, she was not the cure. Blonde pilfered a few handfuls of his best meds (just to keep him from suicide, she told herself), lifted her shimmering hair from the nightstand, and called a taxi for the long, expensive ride home.

I WANT TO TELL you SOME STORIES ABOUT SOME GIRLS I KNOW.
I collect them; the way some people collect stamps or dolls. It always starts with a question, and then it's up to them. You'd be surprised at how easy it is.

I

Well, I'm not really sure if this counts, but it's the thing I remember most.

It was '75 or '76, and I had gone downtown by myself. I was supposed to meet my friend at this record store and then we were going to go hang around together, but I didn't really know where it was. I don't think I had ever been downtown by myself before. I only knew King Street, really, and Main. The rest of Hamilton was pretty much a mystery.

So I'm walking around, not really in a hurry; just looking around. Some guy

Grimsby Girls

said "nice tits" to me and I remember that I was a little bit scared, but I also kind of liked it. It made me feel proud, y'know? Up the street, I saw some guys I knew from school, some friends of my brother's mostly, so I went up to them and asked if they knew where this record store was. They weren't any help, but they were going to some party, so I ended up just tagging along with them. They didn't really know where they were going any more than I did, because they couldn't figure out which house this party was supposed to be at. None of the places on the block had people out front or music or anything, and we ended up knocking on the door of some old lady's house on the corner next to the Mac's Milk. She yelled at us and threatened to call the police, even though we hadn't done anything. I got scared and ran down the alley behind the store. Ken, who I'd known the longest, since he and my

67

brother played hockey together, came back there and told me we had to hide. He tried the door of somebody's Vega and it was open, so we climbed in the back seat and scrunched down. I guess the other guys took off down the road.

Ken moved in closer and made a face and at first I thought he was going to say something, but then I realized that he wanted to fool around. I always liked Ken because he was nice to me when I was just a little kid, and because he had hair like Leif Garrett. I let him touch my boobs and we kind of rubbed up against each other for a while. Then he took it out and put my hand on it. I stroked it and then I spit in my hand and jerked him off. I remember thinking, oh god, if my brother finds out about this I'm dead. When I was done, I asked him, "So are we going out now?" even though I didn't really like him that way. Ken looked at me and started crying. I guess I was okay for a hand job but the thought of going out with me made him cry. I told him I was going to tell my brother that he made me do it but that just made him cry harder. I told him to forget it and that he owed me one. Do you know what he did? He gave me the seven dollars and change he had in his pocket. So I guess that was my fate right from the get-go, because I took it and got out of the car and bought a Tab at the store and a copy of *Creem* magazine and took the bus home and never looked him in the eye again.

But my actual virginity? Well, that I can't tell you. It was at this biker party, but I was pretty into the booze by then and I passed out. It may have even been two or three guys in one night, because I hurt like hell the next day. But I guess it hurts anyway, right?

Of course, not all of them are girls anymore, but they were once. When they tell me, it's like they become girls again. You can see it in their faces, in their eyes. Some of them light right up, and I can imagine them in their girl bodies. Some of them don't light up at all.

II

It was on the beach, but not the way you might envision, because it was at Lake Ontario in November. There was even a bit of snow on the ground. We kept everything on that we possibly could: mittens, coats, boots, everything. I imagine there must have been steam coming off us, because you could certainly see your breath that night. We just couldn't wait any longer, and there was nowhere else for us to go. His parents were Christian, and they wouldn't let us be in his room together with the door closed. My parents didn't even know I had a boyfriend, not after the last one. And I think that's all I'll say about that.

That was his first time, although I was already on the Pill, and once again, that's that. As far as I'm concerned, that night on the beach with the cold and the moon and the frost on the rocks was my first time and it's the time that really counts. I believe that if something goes haywire, a woman gets to erase that and start over. Just once.

Some of these girls might seem too much alike. That can happen. Small towns, and small-town girls, can all start to seem the same after a while. The thing is, I wish every one of their stories could breathe into your ear like an Olivia Newton-John song on the car stereo on a warm summer afternoon. The kind of day where the air is the same temperature as your skin, and being naked feels like swimming. But that's not how it's going to go.

III

It was in my garage, but it's not as bad as it sounds. Okay, it's still pretty bad, but there was a couch in there—it was like my little rec room more than a garage. My parents let me hang out there, because the basement was where they had their bar set up, and the foosball table, plus the spare bedroom, and they needed that space for when they had their card buddies over—not a bunch of stoned teenagers. Which, fair enough, right? It was great when they had friends over on weekends, because they'd hole up down there and get loaded, and never bother us in the garage at all. We could do whatever we liked.

So yeah, it was with a friend of mine, who I'd had a crush on forever, and we were just partying and sitting around one night, talking like we always did, and drawing giant mushrooms and flowers and wizards and stuff on the drywall with magic markers, and then we kissed and ended up on the couch. He was a great kisser, really sexy. Most high school guys didn't kiss like that. He turned me on. We ended up going out for a few weeks, but it turned out to be a bad idea and sex ruined everything. Once we'd been boyfriend and girlfriend, we could never go back to the way things were before. We broke up and could barely look at each other or think of anything to say. I really missed him, because he was a great friend. Sometimes I'd look at his drawings on the drywall—he was a good artist too—and have a little cry about the fun we'd had and how I'd blown our friendship.

These are the girls the big-city radio station makes slut jokes about. Girls grow up in this small town on a lake, and stay and have girls of their own. Sprinklers go titch-titch-titch on green lawns as girls crawl out of their bedroom windows. Ride in cars, up and down Main Street, sneak beers into the park, get finger-fucked behind the school. Every year, only the cars and the outfits are different. Generations of girls mocked on morning radio. Generations of boys in high-school halls daring each another to sniff their fingers.

IV

What? No, no way. I didn't know you were going to ask me that. Honestly, it's none of your goddamn business.

What about the boys? What do they feel, want, need? Are they disappointed? Relieved? Might they be the same as the girls? Why don't I ask them? I'm going to tell you something: I don't care. They've been fucking things for a long time, inanimate objects of every shape, size, and description. A girl is just the holy grail of objects for boys to fuck.

V

I didn't think you could get pregnant the first time, which gives you a clue to how long ago it was. My mother never explained anything about sex to me—the message was just that you didn't do it. For years, I didn't even understand what was supposed to happen—I thought that the man peed inside you. The girls at school sometimes talked about it, but they didn't know any more than I did.

The event itself was…well, it was the way it was. He was pushy and I was scared, and I guess nowadays a girl would go to the police about something like that, but I didn't know any better. We were just going on a date, I thought, and things had gotten out of hand. My biggest worry at the time was that he would tell people and my reputation would be ruined. I didn't know what was in store for me.

A few months later, my parents sent me away to a home for unwed mothers and I had my little girl. They pretty much knocked you out when you had a baby back in those days, so I don't remember much. I guess they might have had battles on their hands if they had let girls see those little babies.

Do I miss her? Well, it's hard to miss someone you've never known. But I do think about it. Sometimes I imagine what it would be like if she came and found me now, but things were such a secret in those days…I don't suppose she got any more information than I did. We just didn't talk about it. When I got back, that was the end of it. I knew people were whispering, but I didn't care. I just wanted to finish school and move away and get a job somewhere where no one knew me. So that's what I did.

Perhaps there's something more timely to communicate here—informa-

tion about teen pregnancy rates, worldwide attitudes on rape, statistics on female genital mutilation. Would that make these stories more important than just looking through a keyhole, like we're doing now?

VI

If you tell anybody about this, you're fucking dead, I swear. Got it? It's happening tonight, after the formal. Dude, I'm serious. Why not? Brandon's older brother put a hotel room on his Visa for us and everything.

Yeah, I think it'll be super-romantic—I mean, we've got the limo until two, and I'm gonna look so hot. Mom thinks I'm staying over at Ashley's, so I even get to sleep in the next day. But mostly I just want to get it over with. It's like when you're waiting for your period to come and it feels like every single girl in your class has it except you and you just want to get it out of the way so you can say that you've had it. Because once that's over with, then you can relax and act normal and shit. I hate that dividing line between who has and who hasn't—I want to get over to the other side. I know it might hurt and it might not even be that great, I don't know. I'm getting totally wasted so I won't feel the pain as much, I hope.

What is it these girls are trying to tell you? Do they want to tell you that sex is painful, sex is boring, sex is nothing like the movies and the romance novels promised? Do they want to tell you that it can be magical sometimes? Do they want to tell you that even when it's not magical, that everything will still be okay?

VII

I haven't lost it yet, if that's the way you want to look at it—as "losing" something. It's not really by choice; I'd like to be in that kind of relationship with someone, I just never figured out how to go about it. And

I didn't want to go around embarrassing myself. Life is hard enough without actively seeking humiliation. I just waited for a nice guy to ask me out, and that never happened. That person just never materialized. I've gone out with girlfriends in the past to a few bars and nightclubs, places like that, and there might have been a couple of opportunities there, but I didn't want to go home with some strange man I met at a bar after last call. How would someone react to that kind of news upon rounding second base: a twenty-seven-year-old woman who's never had sex? Sure, men can say that virgins are "hot," but I think the reality is considerably more awkward than anyone's letting on.

I suppose the worst part is that the longer I'm around, the less likely it seems that the situation will change. It also occurs to me less and less. I've managed this long without it and most of the time I don't understand what the big deal is. I think sometimes about living with another person, having someone to come home to, another warm body in the bed and a kind soul to give me a hug if I've had a bad day, but I don't think about "doing it" that often. If my friends are to be believed, most men are terrible at it anyway. They've all had their hearts broken so often, and for what? I don't know; certainly there's something that keeps them going back for more. But I'm not the one to ask about that.

Now let's just suppose that not all of these girls are real. What if I had made some of them up? Would you be able to tell the difference? Would it matter?

VIII

Oh my god, how embarrassing! It was at a party actually, with my boyfriend. We had been going out for a while, it was probably only a few weeks, but when you're fifteen or sixteen, that's an eternity, isn't it? We had fooled around quite a bit by that point, but we hadn't gotten around to doing it yet. So, we were at this house party of this girl I was friends with, but not best friends or anything. One thing that I remember about her was that she always got to skip school one Friday a month to go and get electrolysis on her moustache and her chin hairs, and she'd always have this reddish face for the rest of the night if you saw her out at the movies or wherever. That's kind of a weird thing for a teenager, eh? Electrolysis? But her parents were quite well off, so it was no big deal for them.

Anyway, the party was at her house, because her parents were on vacation, and of course, everyone loved to go to her parties because she lived in this really nice house on top of a hill and it was close to the high school, so everyone would just meet in the school parking lot and get their drinks organized and wander over from there.

It wasn't like parties you hear about now, where kids come and destroy the house and some poor kid gets stabbed. Did you hear about that? Isn't that awful? My daughter—thank God she wasn't there—heard at school that one of the boys peed right into the top of the father's stereo. Why would anyone do that? I mean, when we were kids, a couple of people would maybe throw up on the carpet or something. And there might be a fight or two, but even that was usually outside on the driveway. We were always so desperate for a place to hang out we were too grateful to trash a place. Besides, why wreck your chances of ever getting to go there again?

Oh, right. So we were at this party, me and my boyfriend Kevin, and we were drinking and dancing. It was really fun. I went to get another drink in the kitchen and there was my ex-boyfriend, Tony. I had broken up with Tony because he was into drugs and it scared me. He hadn't really gotten over me; still leaving little notes in my locker, things like that. Calling my parents' house at all hours and then hanging up, but I knew it was him—and this was way before call display or *69! Anyhow, there Tony was in the kitchen looking very hangdog. I don't remember what exactly he said, but he was so messed up and he kept going on about how pretty I was and how much he missed me. Poor old Tony! Still, I think I had a lucky escape there.

I just wanted to get my beer and get the heck out of there, but Tony blocked my way to the fridge and kept trying to hug me. Then Kevin came in and saw us and got the wrong idea and ran up the stairs and I had to chase after him.

We had a huge fight in the parents' bedroom upstairs, with its black-and-white art posters and a waterbed. It was very glamorous looking, although thinking back on it, it really looked like something out of a sleazy movie! Anyway, I had to convince Kevin that I wasn't interested in Tony anymore. That's when I told Kevin I loved him, and then he said he loved me too and we were so worked up by then...and we'd had a lot to drink! Although if my daughter ever comes to me with that excuse, look out!

It wasn't that bad, all things considered. I'll never forget sloshing around on that waterbed with the velvety bedspread. I guess it could have been more romantic, but I did like him a lot and I was glad that I hadn't wasted myself on Tony. We went out for another two years, almost to the end of high school. Sometimes I still think about Kevin, wondering what he's doing with his life, whether he has kids of his own. I hope so. I hope he's happy.

What I am trying to tell you? There are things I should remember and I don't. I've forgotten some bad things that any sane, any right person would remember happening to them. I'd at least like to say I remember every boy, every name, but I don't. I keep digging around and trying to get the memories out, like a caramel stuck in a bad tooth.

IX

My stepfather raped me when I was thirteen. It went on for about four years, and then I ran away from home.

I'm trying to make a chorus of voices, rising together, but they all just end up sounding like variations of me. My voice looped back and over itself again and again to create the illusion of dimension, like an overproduced pop song.

X

I'm not sure how comfortable I am talking about this, but I will because I think my experience is important. My life as a Christian is essential to me, and I try to live my life in accordance with the Word of God, and that's why I remained pure until marriage and so did my husband. We met at a youth leadership conference several years ago, and there was instantly a connection between us. I think we saw a conviction and a commitment in one another that was very attractive. He told me that he almost didn't go to that conference because he had been considering going overseas to do some missionary work. He says that God obviously had found a partner for him and that's why we were brought together. We dated for just over a year, but they probably weren't the kind of dates a lot of people are used to. We went to prayer group together and met each other's families and began talking about our goals and dreams for the future. I suppose that seems old-fashioned by today's standards, but how else can you get to know someone? It's no wonder there are so many divorces—if you meet someone at a bar and end up marrying them without having any of those discussions, how can you expect anything to last? It was important that Mark and I shared similar ideals: how many children we wanted to have, for example, and the best place to raise them, and how we might serve God as a family, not just as individuals. These are the things that are the foundation of a good Christian marriage, and that's something we took very seriously.

On our wedding day, I felt like I was beginning a new life. Our pastor performed the wedding ceremony and it was wonderful. I did feel a little nervous—I was about to move out of my parents' house and into a brand-new home with my husband, and I knew that night we would be consummating our vows—but I knew that I was making the right decision. I felt truly loved and valued that day, and I was proud to go to our marriage bed as a virgin, to give my body to my husband as a gift in service to the Lord. To say more than that would be wrong.

I've been truly blessed with a loving husband and three wonderful little girls. I know that when the time comes, I'll be talking to my daughters about their bodies and the importance of staying pure. Being a part of this family means not cheapening yourself in God's eyes, and they'll have to follow the example we've set.

I want to tell the girls that you get older and you get sick of things, like girls being half-naked to sell jeans, and movies where the pretty girl dates the ugly loser. I want to warn them to not fake it, to not pretend that something feels good when it doesn't, because really, how fucked up is that? But who wants to listen to my old-woman warnings, my saggy face chewing up words? I am from a thousand years ago.

XI

I met a boy when I was on vacation with my parents in California. I had a boyfriend back home, but he...well, he was really jealous, for starters, and sometimes he'd push me around and things like that. I wasn't very happy, let's just say. So I met this boy when I was out with a couple of other girls one night and he was really nice. His name was Adrian and he took us back to his hotel room, and he and his friends gave us beer. I remember that his parents were in the hotel too, but they let Adrian have his own room. I couldn't believe how lucky he was—they must have been really rich, because it was a fancy hotel too.

After we'd drank all the beer, we went for a walk on the beach and got separated from everyone else because we were walking so slow. We talked about everything: Adrian was from Toronto and went to a private school and never got to hang around with girls, and I told him about my boyfriend and said that I was going to break up with him when I got home. I felt so high when I said that, because I suddenly knew it was true. I didn't have to go out with him anymore, because Adrian was proof that another boy could like me. We started kissing and it felt really good, and I ended up going back to his room with him. Things got pretty heavy, and I kept saying that I'd never done this before—just to make myself feel better—but I think he thought I meant cheating on my boyfriend, not the doing it part. Eventually he told me to shut up and that made me really sad. But for some reason I didn't stop.

When I got back to my parents' hotel room, they were asleep, so I snuck in and went straight to the bathroom and had the hottest shower I could stand. I just sat on the bottom of the tub and cried and let the water fall over me. I felt so dirty and like a bad person. Why wouldn't I have sex with my own boyfriend but I would with this total stranger? He didn't even really seem to like me that much. I kept hearing him saying "shut up" in my head.

We left a couple of days later, and I did break up with my boyfriend as soon as I got home. We went for a drive and I told him I didn't want to go out with him anymore and he got really angry and accused me of going off with other guys. He made me get out of his car right there and drove off and left me on the side of the road. I had to walk the rest of the way home and it took me nearly two hours.

When I started throwing up a couple of weeks later, I just thought I had the flu or something. Then my friend Angela and I bought one of those kits from the drugstore. The worst part was that I couldn't tell anyone about it. I didn't even know Adrian's last name, just that he lived in Toronto somewhere. If I told my parents, they'd think it had been my boyfriend and my dad would have probably killed him or made him marry me or something. And then my boyfriend would have known that I cheated on him and probably would have told the whole school. Every choice I had seemed so awful. I went to the clinic with Angela and everyone was super nice and I told one lady the whole story sitting in her office and crying and she told me what I could do.

So a couple weeks later, Angela borrowed her mom's car and said we were going to the mall and drove me back to the clinic. I was worried that I'd be really sick afterwards but I wasn't. They gave me some Tylenols and we went back to Ange's and just hung out downstairs and watched movies all night. She even sat on the floor so I could have the whole couch to myself.

There are girls waiting their turn, and I can't tell them anything. We have to wait for their stories. Some think it will feel the way kissing does. Some think it will feel the way it does when the boy they like looks at them. Some girls have boys look at them and don't feel anything, but they feel it when they look at their best friends. How long do they have to wait?

XII

I know there are a lot of lesbians who dated men before they came out, or before they even realized they were lesbians. I never had to go through that, since I've known since I was about eleven or twelve, I think. It's not like I ever did anything about it though. Being a teenager was tough. I was just this asexual person until I finally left home for university.

My first time was with a woman I met at a fundraiser. We went to a party afterwards, and I really liked her. She was stunning, and smart, and had the most amazing hips—when she walked, it was just the most gorgeous thing to watch. I think she knew it too. I was nervous as hell, because I'd only recently come out, and I felt like such a baby dyke next to her. But she was great—and of course she knew all about me already. It was such a small scene, like a big extended family with a lot of drama, like any family. But being with her, and we stayed together for many months after that, it gave me a kind of…legitimacy that you can't really underestimate.

We went back to her place that night, and I felt so nervous and awkward, like I wouldn't know what to do. But the moment she touched me, it was like a miracle or something. I can't tell you…how long I'd waited for that moment, and then to have everything make sense, to have every-thing feel right for the first time in your life. Amazing. It was the most in-tense, most powerful connection.

A virgin is her own woman, for good or for ill. After, a part of you belongs to the world, even if you never let anyone in there again. The first time is the only time you don't know how it's going to end, but after that, you'll have plenty of time to understand how it never changes.

XIII

Promise you won't put my name in or anything? Okay. It's kind of gross, though. It happened last summer, at this family barbecue at my Auntie Sheila's. A bunch of my cousins and stuff were there, people I hadn't seen in, like, ten years. It was like a reunion, I guess. My Auntie Sheila's cousin, Rose, was there with her kids, so that makes them my second cousins, I think. They used to live closer to us and we hung out with them more back then. We used to call her Auntie Rose, even though she isn't really our aunt. Her one son, Danny—I had a major crush on him when we were little kids. Our moms would go to the hairdressers together and take us so we could play together. That was back when my mom went to Mrs. White's for haircuts—she had a hair salon in her basement, which I used to think was the coolest thing ever. Her daughter, Tina, was a year older than us, but sometimes she'd play with me and Danny.

I remember this one time, it was Christmas, and Mrs. White had mistletoe hanging in the hallway upstairs and I wanted Danny to kiss me and he made this big deal out of it and made me close my eyes and count to ten and when I did, he leaned in and kissed me, except that I kept my eyes open just a bit and I saw that he'd gotten Tina to do it instead. I was so mad that I punched him and then I got in trouble.

So Danny was at this family thing, and still pretty cute. He looked almost exactly the same, just bigger. I felt all embarrassed, like, if I go over and talk to him, will he still think I'm in love with him? So I tried to act cool about it and just kind of smiled at him. Meanwhile, my mother was being a total spaz and telling me to go over. "Go say hi to Danny! You used to tell me you were going to marry him when you grew up!" I wanted to smack her. He came over a bit later while I was putting mustard on my hotdog. He said, "I've got some ciders in my overnight bag. Come on." So I dumped my Sprite in the grass and went with him and we each drank one really fast in the guest room while he refilled our pop cups. It's not like either of our moms would have noticed anything weird—they were both getting pretty hammered anyway by that time.

We did that twice more, and then he was filling us up one more time and I said, "Did you even have any room left in your bag for clothes?" and he just laughed at me, but a nice laugh, like, you know, I was actually funny. I was glad I had gotten a little bit dressed up that night. I had on my distressed jean skirt and my new black tank top with the lacey straps and my hair was pulled back off my face with a hair band but the rest was still loose.

Later on, when it got dark, most of the old people and the ones with little kids had left and my mom was getting ready to go too. But then Auntie Sheila said Mom was in no condition to drive and we should just stay overnight like Rose's family and we'd all go out for breakfast the next day. Then everyone went inside and watched some stupid video of a trip to Disneyworld, and Danny and me just sat outside, getting bit by mosquitoes and splashing our feet in the pool.

We decided to go for a walk on the golf course and then we sat down under a tree and started kissing. I was stoked to be kissing someone I'd liked for such a long time, even if I had been just a stupid kid. I remembered when he made Tina kiss me and how I was finally getting my wish under the mistletoe. The thing was, he wasn't a very good kisser. His tongue was all big and sloppy, like he'd just kind of unroll into my mouth like a big carpet until I was ready to gag. We were lying down and he put his hand up my skirt and the next thing I know he's on top of me and he's totally going for it, you know? I hoped no one could see us and I tried to be really quiet. It's not like I didn't want to, I just kind of wish I'd had a little more time to think about it. Mostly it just stung, like a rope burn, and it took some trying, to, um, get it in there. But once he did he just went for it for a minute or two and then it was over.

We didn't talk much after that. We walked back to the yard, and I tried to hold his hand, but he pushed it away and looked at me like I was retarded. "What, you want us to get caught?" he said. He did help me pick the grass out of my hair though.

I had to sleep on the pull-out couch in the rec room that night with my mom, which sucked. It sounds stupid, but I was so paranoid that somehow she'd know. I felt so embarrassed the next day I could barely look at anyone, especially Danny. Plus, I had all these grass stains on the back of my skirt. I gave Danny my email at breakfast, but mostly just because Mom told me to.

What I really want to tell you is about how it feels to be entered. What keeps us going back for it is the ache for it, a kind of sickness that's better than the cure. The boys are all different, but the ache is always the same. The urgency shames as much as it thrills.

XIV

Wow, okay. File it under the least romantic thing that's ever happened to me. Well, the first part was fine, but the rest... My boyfriend and I did it in the back seat of his parents' car. He was sixteen and had just gotten his driver's license and I was fourteen. We weren't that far from my parents' house and they were freaking out because I was supposed to be home a couple of hours before and my mother had sent my father out looking for me. So just as we were finishing, I look up to see my father's face peering in the window at us. I screamed it scared me so much. Then I was even more scared, because I thought he might pull us out of the car and kill us. But he just shook his head and walked back to his car and drove away. We cleaned ourselves up and Matt drove me home. He wanted to just drop me off, but I made him go in the house with me.

So that was probably the most awkward conversation I've ever had. My mother kept screaming and being hysterical and my father just stood there looking like he wanted to cry. He didn't really say anything until after Matt went home, and then he just looked at me and said, "You shouldn't even know what it's for except to piss out of." He said if he ever saw me with that boy again, that he'd take off his belt and beat me. He even took off his big brown belt right there in the living room and shook it in my face. He was crying. He'd never laid a finger on me in my whole life, so when he said that, I knew he was serious. But it didn't stop me. Nothing could stop me once I got going.

That last one was mine.

A LOT OF PEOPLE WERE THERE THAT NIGHT, BUT EVERYONE forgets that now. At first, it was about all six of them, who did what to who. It was a group thing, but two of them took it too far. That other guy was there too, at the end, but he gets up on the stand and cries like a baby and now everyone thinks he's a hero. Now, she is all that people see in their minds: her shadow working alone, her shadow in the patchy light under that bridge, her shadow holding that girl under the water. But how do we know? Maybe that girl was already dead. We don't know. It's just her now, in those newspaper pictures in her turtlenecks and dark coats. In the daylight but still a shadow. Always looking down. You'll never catch her crying.

Pen Pal

That's one of the things I like about her. She doesn't give a shit what you think. That, and her dark eyes and her little mouth. She looks like a real Canadian girl to me. Tim Hortons counter, hockey rink, gas station—that kind of girl. I bet she needs a good fuck. Remember, between trials, when she beat up that old lady in the park? She needs a good lay.

She might have gained some weight in the last few years, but it's hard to say. Her shape is hidden under all those dark layers. Her face for sure looks rounder, but that could just be age. Some girls get like that. Her hair is shorter; it stops at her shoulders. I still have the newspaper clippings from before, when it was longer. Those sunny days when she'd walk into the courthouse wearing her cream-coloured sweater and her shiny brown hair would fan out behind her. Like a wind machine was blowing. Cameras going off all around her like she was a movie star.

Just saying her name makes my balls hurt.

That other girl, the one who died, probably didn't deserve it. In the stories I saved, the newspapers talked about what a loser she was. Didn't have many friends, didn't get along with her parents. Her ugly face in the school photo staring out. I cut those pictures out and threw them away, because they made me feel bad. I don't want to think about that.

I've written her letters, not coming on too strong. Just being friendly and asking how she is, stuff like that. I haven't heard anything back yet, but it's okay. Where's she going to go? One day she'll get lonely, and that's when I'll be there. I'll visit her in jail, and she'll meet me and see I'm serious. If I'm allowed, I can even bring some stuff: shampoo and magazines; things girls like. After a while, she'll start calling me her boyfriend. We'll be able to have those visits in the trailer. I imagine her in her bra and panties, her thin lips glossy and smiling. She's ready for me. She's been waiting for this for a long time.

Every time we do it, she wants to be on top. I'm okay with that. I like to just lie there and look at her while she rides me. But sometimes, when I'm close, she puts her hands around my throat and her eyes get squinty and I haven't breathed in what seems like a long time and my chest burns and I start seeing sparkles and I think I'm afraid. But then I'm bursting with come inside her and she leans back and takes her hands off and laughs and laughs and laughs.

I'M GOING UP THE STAIRCASE ON ALL FOURS. IT'S QUIET IN the back part of the house, except for some people I can hear talking in the hallway above me. I go slow; for a few moments I can almost imagine I'm alone. The stairs are wood, and slippery on my sock feet, and I'm too drunk to risk wiping out. I've never been good at going up stairs for some reason. I even have this scar on my lip, here, from when I tripped up our basement steps when I was a little kid. So I use my hands. My hair hangs down on either side of my face. I like how wavy and orange it looks.

The Devil You Know

I hope there's no one in the bathroom when I get there. I just need to sit on the floor for a couple of minutes, maybe rest my face on the cold edge of the bathtub. A drink of water from the sink and splash my face a bit. There's bound to be a hairbrush, some mouthwash, maybe a little perfume. Then I'll feel better. Maybe I'll even jerk off. I love doing that in other people's bathrooms at parties. I don't know why; it just gives me a thrill I guess. And it always makes me feel more awake. I do it at work sometimes, too, when I'm on my break, but it's riskier there, with the stalls and everything.

I just need a minute away from everyone. I don't even know where Rhonda is, and it's her house. The kitchen is packed; everyone shoving and laughing and shouting and lighting sambucas and almost setting the counters on fire. Man, those sambucas were a bad idea. I don't even like licorice. Lighting it on fire doesn't make it taste any better.

My hands wrap around the carpeted edge of the top step and I pull myself up on the banister. I don't feel as bad as I expected. But the bathroom door is closed, and there's light bleeding out onto the carpet from underneath it. Shit. I lean against the wall and smile at the other people in the hall. I hope they haven't been laughing at me. There's Lauren. She waves me over. I push off the wall and it feels as though I'm moving through honey.

A guy with a tan face smiles at me. His teeth are huge and luminescent. His white shirt looks like it's glowing too. I look at his glowing arm and there's a joint in his hand, which I take. I've had more than enough downstairs, but I'm not going to refuse. This might sound stupid, but it's kind of a pride thing with me. If I get offered something, I take it, no matter what. It's called being reliable, not just some dumb high-school girl who can't keep it together. I can always accidentally lose a drink I can't finish, or even throw it up later if I need to. Drugs are harder to fake, so I usually end up getting pretty fucked up. But that's one of the reasons I get to go to these parties, even though nearly everyone's at least ten years older than me. That, and the fact that I like to fuck.

I take a hit and pass it to Lauren. She smiles and shakes her head and her eyes are glittering in that catlike way they do when she's really high. It's like she can see your insides working. She takes a picture of me with her phone. I make a mental note to swipe it and delete it later.

The tan guy smiles again and says, "I'm Kyle. Who are you?"

"Cynthia," I say. "Thanks for the weed."

Kyle grins. "Oh, it's better than that."

And wouldn't you know it, as if by magic, the weirdest feeling comes up through my feet and legs and up my body and then out the top of my head. It takes stuff with it too, like my balance. The edges of the world go all rubbery, and I feel like I'm on a boat heading over a waterfall. There's a burst of light on my right as the bathroom door opens, and I start to walk over there without feeling my feet touch the floor. I once stayed up for almost three days straight partying in Toronto and had the exact same feeling. I get in and close the door and lie down on the tiles, just to get my shit together for a second. I can hear a lot of voices, but I don't know where they're coming from.

The next thing I see is Tyler, asking if I'm okay. I get kind of offended. "I've only been in here for a couple minutes," I say, my tongue feeling too big for my mouth.

"Baby, you've been in here for over an hour," he says.

I don't believe him. He helps me stand up and we walk over to the sink. I look in the mirror and see that I've got bits of lint and hair and stuff from the floor stuck to my cheek. I splash some water on my face and scrub it with a towel. "I need to go outside," I say.

"It's really cold out."

"Don't care."

I'm really wobbly, so Tyler helps me down the steps like I'm his grandma. I'm sliding all over the place in my socks. We go through the kitchen, where there are still a lot of people, and onto the back porch. The air is really cold and I'm hoping it will clear the cotton candy out of my head, but I just feel cold and crappy. I start to shiver. I lean over the railing to throw up, but before I do, I look back through the screen door to the kitchen and see that Kyle guy standing by the sink. He's grinning at me.

For the rest of the night, I'm on the couch in the spare room with a holey afghan over me, barfing into a plastic bowl. Tyler stays with me, thank god, bringing me water and emptying the bowl and patting me on the shoulder. Rhonda comes in at one point and tries to get me to drink some maple syrup to fix my brain sugar, she says, but I can't do it. I can't stop shaking, and every time I try and close my eyes, I get the spins right away. It's one of those nights where you want to sleep so bad that you wish you were dead. Worst March break ever. In the window, I keep seeing faces floating outside, even though I know they're not there because we're on the second floor. The sky behind the faces turns light grey with morning before I finally stop trembling and doze off. The last floating face I see is Kyle, his tan face and dark eyes and white teeth, smiling at me.

✻　✻　✻

On Wednesday, four days after Rhonda's party, Cynthia took a phone call from a number she didn't recognize. It was Kyle.

"I got your number from Rhonda," he said. "We met at the party this weekend."

"I remember," she said. She had seen the picture Lauren took with her cell, and begged her to delete it. Her eyes looked they were pointing in two different directions.

"I wasn't sure if you would," he said and chuckled.

She waited for him to apologize for making her sick.

"I want to know if you'll go for dinner with me this Saturday."

"Really? Uh, I guess so," she said.

"I'll pick you up at seven," he said. He took her address down. "See you then," he said. "Wear something nice."

Cynthia, like most of her friends, had never gone on what could properly be called a date. It seemed to her like something her grandparents or the teenagers in *Archie* comics did. People hooked up with people at parties and either ended up going out with them or not. For her first real date, she tried on about five outfits, and decided on her dark skinny jeans and grey silk top and her black boots.

Kyle pulled up to the house in a new red Mustang, a total douche-mobile, but a decent car. Her last boyfriend hadn't had a car at all, which made things difficult. Cynthia didn't have her license yet, and she wasn't in a hurry to get it. She'd failed two driver's tests already, and on her second try, had nearly run over a Dalmatian that darted in front of the car. The test itself seemed to turn her into a bad driver, even though she had plenty of experience behind the wheel. One older boyfriend she'd gone out with for a while was such a drunk that she'd nearly always end up driving them both home from the bar in his little Toyota pickup. But she liked being the passenger and not having to worry about getting drunk or paying for gas. A good fake ID and no license was a good combination for a seventeen-year-old.

"You look nice," he said.

"Thanks. I like your car," she lied.

"Yeah, you like cars?"

"I like going places in them."

He drove fast, which wasn't surprising. They went to The Keg, where Cynthia had only been on her birthday. They both had steaks with shrimp on top, and garlic mashed potatoes, and the salad bar, and a basket full of bread. After dinner, Kyle ordered a Crown Royal on the rocks. Cynthia panicked and asked for the only liqueur she could think of—crème de menthe. Her mother had been on a kick of pouring it over vanilla ice cream for dessert.

Kyle laughed at her choice. "You like that stuff?"

"Sure—gets you drunk while it freshens your breath."

He smiled.

"And it tastes good when you barf too," she said, snorting.

He frowned.

"Sorry."

They talked about her high school a bit, people he might remember from when he'd been there. He'd graduated five years before, but he knew her friend Kayla's ex-boyfriend Justin. He knew that the French teacher was a drunk, but he hadn't heard that he and one of his students had run off together. He told Cynthia that he worked for a landscaping company, but his hands didn't look rough or dirty. He didn't ask her what she wanted to do after high school, to her relief, since she had no idea.

In the parking lot of the restaurant, he took her hand and nodded across the street at the neon sign of the Lakeview Motor Hotel. "Want to get a room for the night?"

She grinned at him, but his face was serious.

Cynthia nodded. She liked it when people were clear.

❋   ❋   ❋

She looked at the maps and brochures in the dusty display rack while Kyle checked them in. It was strange to look at pamphlets for Marineland and Niagara Falls as a tourist might. She tried to imagine being someone from far away, deciding to take a vacation and then deciding to take that vacation here, of all the places in the world a person could choose.

Kyle wasn't much of a kisser; he pressed too hard and pushed his pointed tongue into her mouth. His body was as hard as his mouth, but that was different. He had a smooth chest and his butt had those little dents in the sides and there was a line of muscle where his abdomen turned into his narrow brown hips. Naked, he looked like an underwear model or one of the firemen on her mother's calendar. Cynthia lay beneath him as he fucked her and wondered if he'd be better the next time. Maybe he wouldn't press so hard on everything. Of course, she considered, there might not be a next time. Checking into a hotel on your first date could either be the beginning or the end. It didn't really matter either way. She wondered if he'd want her to be his girlfriend. She had been trying to take a few weeks off from guys, but it wasn't easy. They just kept popping up, and she never said no. She thought about sex while she examined her fingernails over his shoulder. She'd never understood how she was supposed to hold off from sex, and found it bizarre how some of her friends could go out with someone for weeks without it. How did that work? Once Cynthia started making out, she didn't understand how to stop. Where was the line? Was the line determined beforehand, or during? She understood how a person might not feel like having sex, but couldn't think of a time for herself that it had seemed worth stopping. It was, at the very least, an interesting experiment. Or just something to do. What else was there to do, once everything had been said?

She squeezed her muscles inside, like she'd read in *Cosmopolitan*, as he came inside her, and it occurred to her that she hadn't told him she was on the Pill.

They slept on and off, waking up and talking for a while, then fucking again. In the morning, she felt sore and overrubbed. She looked at his body as he dressed. He was sexy, probably the sexiest guy she'd ever been with. She wondered if this was how men felt looking at women.

He saw her watching him. "Get up, lazy," he said, smiling and pulling off the sheet, "and let's get some breakfast." While she found her underwear and pulled on her jeans, he chopped up a couple of squat lines on the glass-topped desk and motioned her over. She tried to look cool doing hers.

They ate in the hotel coffee shop. He had steak and eggs, and she had silver dollar pancakes and a side order of peameal bacon, which she barely touched. Her legs jiggled under the table like a little kid's.

They listened to the Howard Stern Show on satellite radio as he drove her home. When she gathered her things to leave the car, he put his hand on her thigh and said, "I had a good time."

"Me too," she said.

"Can I call you again?"

She grinned. "Uh-huh."

❋   ❋   ❋

Kyle called Cynthia sometime after eight every Wednesday night to make plans for the coming Saturday, the only night of the week they spent together. The call was always short, and they never talked on any other night, not even a text. He picked her up at her parents' house in his Mustang, and was always on time. He didn't come to the door, just gave one brief honk, even though she could hear the car's engine from about three blocks away. It made her father angry.

"Is this friend of yours ever planning to come to the door like a goddamn human being?" her father asked, as Cynthia put on her jacket.

"In my day, a boy had to come in the house and talk to a girl's parents before he was allowed to take her out on the town," he said as she took her keys from the bowl on the counter.

"Oh please, Kevin," her mother groaned from her spot on the sofa. The coffee table was covered in her scrapbooking supplies. She was working on a page about her trip to Vegas last year with a group of other moms. Cynthia had seen the pictures: embarrassing shots of middle-aged women in ill-fitting club clothes. Yellowed teeth and muffin tops. Umbrella cocktails and too many accessories.

"I'm staying out tonight, so don't expect me back," Cynthia said.

"Oh don't worry, we never do," said her mother with a dismissive wave, a martini-shaped sticker on the end of her ring finger.

※　※　※

Every week, they went out for dinner and drinks, and then to a hotel. Fucking and drugs, breakfast and home. Kyle paid for everything and decided everything. The restaurant, the hotel, what beer to buy. One week he surprised her.

"Where do you want to go for dinner?"

"Oh! Um, okay. Do you like curry? How about that Indian place near the mall?"

"I'm not eating any Paki food."

She laughed, but his cheeks looked warm. "Ohhhh-kay then," she said.

"It stinks, is all. I just don't like the smell and when you eat it, you smell—"

"Let me guess, like a Paki?"

He took her to the new Chinese buffet place instead. They had everything, not just Chinese food, and it was all you could eat. Cynthia was going to make a joke about all the waitresses being white, but thought she'd better not. She didn't want to spoil their night out.

That night, in the hotel room, he sat down on the bed and handed her a small velvet box. Inside was a delicate gold chain with a gold cross pendant.

"Wow. This is really nice," she said.

"Do you like it?"

"I do." Cynthia had never considered herself a religious person, but the necklace was pretty. She took it from the box and had Kyle fasten the chain around her neck. "Thank you."

"I want you to wear it and think of me, okay?"

"Okay," she said, and kissed him.

❉   ❉   ❉

Lauren sent her a text just before lunch on Thursday.

did u knw kyle is a totl dealer??

r u high?

4 real! kayla sez justin knws

ok lies

hes wierd tho and u nevr hang wit us on sat nites anymore

sorry. c u at lunch k?

luv u u knw

i knw

❉   ❉   ❉

At lunch, Cynthia promised Lauren that she'd bring Kyle out the next Saturday, since it was already after they'd made their date for the week. "You'll see—he's really nice. He gave me this," she said, pointing at the gold cross.

"Yeah, that's totes your style."

"Don't be mean."

"Okay, but I just want to know. Why does he only go out with you on Saturdays and then not talk to you for the rest of the week?"

"I don't know. After all, you'd think that'd be a dealer's busiest night, right?"

"Okay. Forget it. How does Tyler feel about this, anyway?"

"Stop trying to force-feed me Tyler. It's not going to happen."

"Why not? He sooo loves you."

"Because he smells like an old towel and I'm already dating someone else. God!"

"Well, I'll make sure he doesn't get the invite for Saturday then."

"Thank you very much."

❋ ❋ ❋

Cynthia knew Kyle liked her red hair, so she hennaed it every other Friday afternoon to really bring out the colour. She mixed the green-brown powder into a coarse sandy paste, packed it onto her head, and tied a grocery bag tightly over it. She'd leave it in for a couple hours, even while she ate dinner, which her father thought was disturbing. It got hot under the plastic, and sometimes she'd sweat and it would mix with the henna and run down her forehead. Then she'd have to scrub the brownish red border from around her hairline. But it was all worth it when he wound his hands up in it and lifted it off her neck and bit at the pale flesh of her freckled shoulder.

"So fucking gorgeous," he said. She loved it when he said that.

❋ ❋ ❋

Another Saturday night, another hotel room. This one was funny because it was kind of seedy. The television and the telephone were both bolted to their tables, which made her laugh, and there were iron-red stains around the drain of the bathtub and the sink, which was more gross than funny. Cynthia looked at the stains on the stucco ceiling as he thrust into her. He pulled out and motioned her to turn over. She flipped onto her hands and knees and braced herself with a pillow. But he took his cock and pressed it against her anus. She leapt forward and smacked her head on the headboard. "Hey!" she said, rubbing her crown.

"Hey what?"

"Well, um, you surprised me there."

"You don't like that?" he teased, shaking his penis at her.

"I, I don't know. I don't think so."

"Why not? Have you ever tried it?"

"I don't need to try something to know I don't like it," she said, inching away and gathering an edge of the sheet.

"That's not very open-minded of you."

"Neither's not eating curry."

"Baby, those are two things that should never be in the same conversation."

"Can we just go back to doing what we were doing?"

"Sure. You want a little more coke?"

Back at it, he kept a thumb pressed against the hole, and she shuddered. The coke helped her feel a bit better about it, but she'd never want a dick in there. She knew this was a thing for lots of guys, but that was just disgusting. After he was done, she hustled to the bathroom and put it out of her mind. She turned the taps on and brought herself to orgasm quickly by watching herself in the mirror. Kyle had never made her come, but so far no one had. Cynthia was okay with taking care of it herself, and she didn't like to offend by saying anything.

※ ※ ※

Cynthia's lips were turning numb, which made the application of fresh gloss a sloppy affair. She made faces at herself in the bathroom mirror of the Pumphouse. She pursed them at her reflection and made farting sounds, all to delay her return to the table, where things were not going well. Kyle had been surly all night, and Cynthia's friends were obviously sizing him up unfavourably. Cynthia had been working her way through the cocktail list to steady her nerves, and now they were all jumbled up together in her stomach, Bloody Caesars careening off raspberry shooters and a bunch of buffalo chicken wings floating around in the brew. This made her laugh, thinking of whole chicken wings bobbing around in her stomach like little boats. She swayed back to the table.

"What took you so long?" asked Kyle, not looking at her.

"I had to take my chicken-wing boats out for a spin. Here chicky, chicky, chicky…"

"I have no idea what you're talking about."

"S'nothin. Doesn't matter." But she kept laughing and snorting.

He glared at her, and she noticed how small his eyes were. "Grow up, for Christ's sake," he hissed.

"Did you know that you have really small eyes?" she asked. "Wittle itty bitty eyes. And how do you get so tan all the time? Do you go to a fake and bake?" Everyone at the table was watching them.

"That's it, we're going." He pulled her to her feet and nodded to the circle of frowns.

Cynthia blew exaggerated kisses. "See you later, fuckfaces," she slurred.

She nearly tripped on the steps outside the bar and Kyle caught her arm and held it tight. "Ow, you're hurting me."

"Then stop acting like a goddamn kid. What the hell's the matter with you?" He climbed into the car without getting the door for her the way he usually did. Inside, she tried to turn on the radio. He slapped her hand away. "Don't touch my car."

"You're being a jerk. Why are you so mean?" she asked as he drove.

"You're drunk," he said.

"So what? That doesn't mean anything. That doesn't mean that I'm not telling the truth or that you're not mean because you are. You are."

"Oh yeah? You want to see mean?"

She shook her head.

"You think I go out with you so we can hang out with your stupid bitchy girlfriends and watch you get drunk and scream and act like a spoiled brat?"

Kyle turned off the highway a couple roads before hers. He drove down a dead-end side road, where a house had been under construction for months.

"What are we doing?"

"You can't go home yet. It's only ten-thirty. You're a fucking mess— you want your parents to see you like this?"

"No. Stop being mean to me," she said quietly.

"C'mere." He reached over her and pulled the seat lever and it reclined. He climbed over the gearshift onto her seat and got on top of her. He pushed her leggings down with one hand and held himself up with the other, pressing down on her shoulder and pinning her hair so Cynthia couldn't turn her head. She felt a bit dizzy lying on her back, but tried not to get the spins. She remembered that Kayla had told her the way she avoided the spins when she was drunk was to really concentrate on her breathing, like yoga or something. Inhale and exhale.

She didn't say anything. He didn't kiss her, just pushed inside. He always got so hard so fast. It stung for a while, then she began to get wet in spite of herself. She listened to his breathing and looked out over his shoulder through the windshield, to the new leaves on the trees. Inhale and exhale.

※　※　※

On Friday night, Tyler came over to watch a movie with Cynthia. She put on her henna right before he arrived. She didn't care if Tyler saw her with a bag on her head. He'd already seen her barf in a bowl. After the movie, she made some instant coffees and they sat in her bedroom with the windows open so she could smoke his cigarettes.

"How are things with you and Kyle?"

"Okay, I guess."

"You guys have been going out for a while now."

"Yeah, it's been a couple of months. It's okay."

"Just okay?"

"Yeah. I don't know. He's nice. We don't have a lot to talk about though. I just feel like it's not going anywhere. I thought that's what I wanted, though, you know? I just wanted to be able to do my own thing and not have some guy in my business all the time and Facebook-stalking me. But now it just seems kind of random. Just going out once a week and eating dinner and getting drunk and then going to a hotel."

"You guys stay in a hotel every Saturday?"

"I like hotels."

"No, I didn't mean to—"

"It's okay."

"I just meant, doesn't he have his own place?"

"He does, yeah, but it's a really small apartment and he shares it with this other guy, Geoff, who's super creepy. I've only been there a couple times, just to pick something up, and he always looks at me really psycho." She changed the subject, because she didn't want to think about Geoff and his bloodshot eyes, or the times they'd gone by just to pick up more coke. "Actually, last week? We went back to Kyle's parents' house and I stayed in the guest room overnight, which was kind of...interesting."

"What were his parents like?"

"Nice. His mom made breakfast and everything. They asked me all these questions about school and stuff and said I seemed really smart and that Kyle had finally 'met his match,' whatever that means." She lit a new cigarette off the cherry of the old one.

"Maybe he usually goes out with dumb girls."

"I guess. But the thing is, at the time, it made me feel happy, right? Like, I want his parents to like me and stuff. But afterwards, I was like, do I even want to be this person's match?"

"I don't get it."

"Yeah, me neither, really. Like I said, I thought that everything was awesome at first, and now...now it just makes me kind of sad, or bored, or...I don't know what."

"Hmm." He blinked owl-like over the tops of his glasses.

"Oh, Tyler, if I haven't figured any of this shit out by the time I'm twenty, can I just marry you?"

"Thanks a lot." He rolled his eyes.

"No, you know what I mean!" she said, punching his arm. "We're just friends and I love you. But if things don't work out for either of us... We get along, right?"

"Yeah. We do."

"So it's a deal. Smoke the rest of this one. I gotta go rinse this crap off my head."

✳   ✳   ✳

Kyle drove with the windows open on one of the first really warm nights in June. Cynthia made waves in the air with her cupped hand. They ate fish and chips down by the pier and watched kids eating ice cream, old couples in sun hats, and teenagers wandering the edges of the darkening park. They drove some more, out to the Travelodge by the closed amusement park. A weathered sign promised future waterslides. Some travelling sports team was also staying at the hotel, drinking and laughing and running up and down the hallway. Kyle couldn't figure out the air conditioner and wouldn't want to call the front desk for help. He jammed the back door of their room open with his shoe and the screen door let in a wisp of cooler air from the lake beyond the courtyard. Cynthia slept naked and fitfully in the heat, sweating into the stiff sheets and the strange pillow. She didn't know how many hours had passed when she woke, struggling out from under suffocating dreams to the sound of whispering. She tried to piece together what she was hearing and where it was coming from. Kyle lay snoring beside her. She opened her eyes a slit. Through the screen door, the shapes of bodies materialized. Men's bodies, standing together on the other side of the screen door, looking at her. Whispering. Cynthia couldn't hear what they were saying, but she sensed that they were making a decision. They seemed to be arguing. She heard a voice say, "Fuck that, bro. I'll do it," before he was shushed. One of them produced a flashlight.

Cynthia acted as though she were dreaming and rolled over and kicked Kyle behind the knees. He did not stir. She rolled over again, winding her body up in a corner of the sheet. The men outside inhaled collectively and took a half-step backwards. It was enough of an opening. She sat upright and screamed. The sound was higher and longer than anything she could have believed.

In their new room, with the working air conditioner and good locks, Cynthia took the tablet that Kyle gave her and lay down on the bed. She left all her clothes on and waited for the blackness of the pill to take her. Sleep came, and she dreamt of Mr. Mugs, the shaggy sheepdog from her Grade One readers, but in her dreams he was gigantic and covered in blood and pieces of bone and tendon. Mr. Mugs was eating everyone. He ate the sweaty hotel manager and those boys at the door and the angry coach and Kyle. He was eating them all, and then he came for her, and no sound would come out of her mouth, and even though she clung to the headboard, she could not stop being pulled into the dog's huge mouth, a dark red cave pouring blood.

❋   ❋   ❋

Epilogue

I'm standing at the far end of the attic, where the ceiling is low. The tall people get stuck standing in the middle. It's getting crowded and loud and hot, everyone drinking and laughing and swaying to the music. The attic makes the house even better for parties now that it's finished. I used to sneak up here sometimes when it was just an attic, though, so I'll miss doing that. Rhonda's sitting in the corner, reading people's tarot cards. She read mine earlier and said that Kyle and I were meant to be together. I've hardly even seen her lately, so I don't know how she knows anything about it. She's probably just mad because he might not come around and bring her coke anymore. Of course, he's here somewhere. I haven't seen him yet, but Lauren told me.

I decide to go out on the roof. It used to be a lot harder to do, but the new skylight makes it easy. I open the hatch and pull myself through, then brace my feet on the frame and walk up the slope to the flat part. As soon as I stand up, I see Kyle already standing there. Shit.

He looks small compared to the sky behind him and all the lights in town.

"Sorry," I say. "I didn't know you were out here."

"It's okay. Don't go back in."

I sit down on the edge of the roof over the street, and he comes and sits beside me. Our feet dangle in the air, and I look across the road to the shoe-repair shop and the barber's and the laundromat and the post office. The laundromat glows with yellow light; it's open until eleven. I can see the bottom half of a woman in pink leggings loading a dryer.

I feel like I should say something. "Sometimes I want to jump," I say. He looks at me. "Not actually jump, but you know. That urge you get? Like you might be able to fly or something."

"Why are you breaking up with me?" is what he says.

"I'm not. Well, I guess I sort of am. I'm sorry."

"But why? What did I do?"

"Nothing. You've been really nice." All those dinners and drinks. The cross on a chain in my jewellery box.

"Is it another guy?"

"No, no one." This is the first time I've said this and meant it, I think. For a second I see Tyler in my head, but there's no sickening guilt to go with it.

"Do you think we might get back together?"

This surprises me. He looks like a kid, sitting there with his sad face. There's a second where I consider trying to explain how I'm feeling. How I was bored and scared at the same time. How I felt when he was fucking me, like I hated it, but I was grateful anyway and didn't know why. How what I want is something that doesn't feel like work all the time, or explaining everything, or trying to guess what's going on. I'm not sure that's even a real thing, a possible thing. But I just shake my head.

"We met here, remember?" he says. "I thought you looked so beautiful."

I do remember—how fucked up I got, and how he laughed at me when I barfed. "I liked your teeth," I say.

"Listen, Cyn," he says, stroking my hair. "If we really are breaking up, and we're not going to get back together…"

I have a shiver of fear, like maybe he's going to push me off the roof and tell everyone I fell.

"Would you mind giving me one last blow job? You're so good at it."

It feels like when the coyote from the cartoons steps off the cliff, and his legs go around really fast and he stays in mid-air for a while. Like there's nothing under my feet. I shake my head, but I smile. I stand up and say, "See you later," and walk back to the skylight. I feel kind of sick, but also very tall. It's weird.

Stars, hide your fires;
Let not light see my black and deep desires
–Macbeth

I'VE BEEN A LIAR ALL MY LIFE. NOT JUST TYPICAL CHILDISH lies to avoid the consequences of my actions, but elaborate fabrications of my imagination, often based on a story of personal victimization. In the fifth grade, I convinced my schoolyard chums that I was being molested by an uncle. I don't know where this idea came from, but it seemed so delicious and dramatic in the telling. Of course, my story was tempered by an incomplete understanding of what "molestation" meant, but it was sufficient to enthrall a group of ten-year-olds.

Soft Limits

The habit of lying for the purposes of a good story has never left me. While I no longer lie awake at night inventing horrible scenarios to recount in the girls' washroom, the small lies I tell each day, each week, soon pile up like psychic snow. Fabrications made in the moment are consistently more interesting than the truth, and they still feature me as one of life's little victims. Example: at the coffee shop yesterday, the barista commented she had missed me the day before for my usual three o'clock latte. Instead of telling her I had been at the dentist, I made up a story about going for a pap smear because they found abnormal cells the last time. What purpose, I ask you, does this serve? Why upset the nice young woman who makes my coffee? Why would I share this information with someone who is essentially a stranger, even if it were true, which it is not? And why, more often than not, do I employ my own body in these narratives—giving it, if you will, any number of illnesses and injuries, just in the service of my lies?

I have no answers. What is certain is that I have grown increasingly disconnected from the world around me. While I maintain an appearance of optimism and joie de vivre, inside there is a void. It's possible that when one presents a false self to the world, the real self begins to fade, to slip away. From my highlighted hair to my padded brassiere to the degree that appears on my résumé, which I am actually four courses shy of receiving, my entire identity is a construct. It's hardly surprising that I have few real friendships, and nothing long-lasting in the romantic department. (In high school, I told my first boyfriend that my mother beat me with a yardstick, not anticipating that he would get drunk and confront her and very nearly push the poor woman down a flight of stairs.) I am beginning to feel adrift—as though I am scarcely connected to humankind at all. Hamlet's "weary, stale, flat, and unprofitable" world springs to mind.

It should be noted that I have had every advantage in life, and that I am well aware of my own good luck. I am in reasonably good health, not unattractive, and have a well-paying and comparably secure job working in communications for a large public service. I was born into a middle-class family, am on good speaking terms with my parents, and make the mortgage payments on my condominium without undue hardship.

Though I am loath to admit it, I have read a number of self-help books recently in an attempt to shake off this cloak of misery. In the short term, which is to say over the weekend while I'm reading them, I feel as though change is within my grasp. I have sat down on Sunday nights and made my to-do list for the week with renewed enthusiasm. Like that oft-clichéd phoenix, I shall rise from the ashes of my many failings. Incompleted projects and soured romance, missed fitness classes and fast-food hamburgers, all will be blown away by the breeze. I will spring fully formed into the dawn of a Monday morning, living a new day, in which there is ample time for all my desires and not a moment of life's precious gift misspent: exercise taken, sensible meals prepared and eaten, reading, fresh air, pleasure and efficiency in my work, time for family and friends, a clean home.

Of course, any good plan must allow for contingencies and forgiveness. Those Monday mornings turn into days and afternoons and weeks filled with circumstances beyond one's control, and after trying to accept the things one cannot change, it becomes clear that the book's author did not allow for the possibility that the universe will beat one down the moment one's back is turned.

Soon enough, I'm leaving the bookshop with my latest purchase tucked under my arm as though I'm smuggling pornography. But now, even the hopeful dreams promised on its dust jacket ring false. Only halfway through Sunday, I can smell the failures of another week approaching. I am doomed, it appears, to repeat this same pathetic charade without ever changing at all.

※　※　※

I have not been sleeping well. My physician, hesitant to prescribe sleeping pills, advised me to try Gravol as an occasional sleep aid. I'm now punching half a dozen of these tablets through their crackly tinfoil shells each night. The no-name brand offers considerable savings. I divide my purchases between the three pharmacies in proximity to my home. I have also lost a great deal of weight in a relatively short time. The depression diet, I suppose. I was quite unaware of the changes in my body until I put on a pair of slacks one morning and they slid off my hips as I walked to the kitchen. A rare gaze into the full-length mirror behind my closet door revealed the physique of a person requiring some medical attention.

Each morning, when I wake up, I have about thirty seconds of feeling well. I'm awake; the sun is streaming through my blinds; the bed is soft and warm and comfortable. Then a cloud covers my thoughts, as I slowly realize all the things to be unhappy about. Then I don't wish to be awake and roll over, hoping for more sleep, which seldom comes. I rise and begin the joyless enterprise of getting ready for work.

※　※　※

And yet. There is something—someone, specifically. A cook, of all things, at the greasy spoon where I sometimes eat lunch when I need to escape the stifling office environment. I went there only days ago, to eat something eggy, try and coax a bit of nourishment into myself. (My work skirts are so large they spin around my waist as I walk, the back vent eventually working its way around to the front.) When I'd finished my omelette, a hand took the plate away and replaced it with a smaller plate on which sat a slice of lemon meringue pie. I looked up to tell the waitress I hadn't ordered it, only to see a man in a white apron.

"This is on the house," he said.

I shook my head, but he shook his head back at me and I could immediately see he would brook no argument. "You've lost too much," he said, flicking his head at my frame. "A little extra looks good on you."

"Is that so?" I said, ready to instruct him on the correct way to address his customers, but then he grinned and I confess, it was quite disarming. Then he turned and walked back through the swinging silver doors of the kitchen.

When I went to the front counter to settle the bill, the server told me that "Troy" had taken care of it. At first I thought she just meant the pie and moved to correct her, but she insisted it was the entire meal.

※　※　※

For some reason—my own curiosity and outrageous vanity, I suppose—I returned the next day for a cup of coffee and a bowl of rice pudding. They make a lovely homemade rice pudding, with none of those vile bloated raisins to spoil it. Sure enough, halfway through my coffee, Troy came out to refill my cup. I felt pathetically obvious.

"Mind if I sit down for a second?"

"Not at all. I wanted to thank you for yesterday. It wasn't necessary."

"I know." He smiled a big wholesome smile at me. His shoulders seemed nearly as wide as my peripheral vision would allow. Thick neck,

close-cropped hair, ruddy cheeks. He looked like a Polish settler, ready
to construct a prairie homestead, not flip burgers in a downtown diner.
A farm girl's dream. But his expression was sweet and gentle. "I would
like," he said, resting his broad hands on the table on either side of me,
"to take you to a movie on Friday night."

※　※　※

We went to a Hollywood blockbuster, the sort of thing I usually abhor, but
I said nothing, happy enough to have gotten out of the house. Within moments of the coming attractions, Troy placed his hand on my knee. It crept
up my thigh through the first act, making it difficult to concentrate.
Luckily, the movie asked little of the viewer, so instead I sat wondering
what to do. What had brought this on? Why was this man interested in
me? Why was I responding to his overtures? Had I become desperate in
my loneliness? He slipped his other arm around me and pulled me
close. As though reading my thoughts, he whispered, "Just relax." I usually hate being told to relax, but I decided that being tense and over-
thinking the situation in a darkened theatre when I could be watching a
film and eating from a shared box of Junior Mints was in fact, silly.

We went out for a drink afterwards, and under the table, Troy caressed
the inside of my thigh. I must admit, the sensation was pleasurable, but I
felt ridiculous and juvenile. I worried that we would be spotted carrying
on. The drinks worked a strange spell on me, though, and I allowed him
to continue.

He said he wanted to walk me to my apartment, so I let him. Then
outside my apartment, he said he wanted to come in. I let him in. He kissed
me before I'd even removed my shoes, and without exaggeration, picked
me up in his arms like a bride and carried me into my own bedroom. I
could not believe this was happening, yet there was something so romantic,
so—and I assure you I am cringing even as I say this—*masterful* about it. I
felt like an overcome heroine in his arms, and his kisses were bold and

persuasive. I am fully aware this sounds like the penultimate scene in some paperback bodice-ripper novel, but there it is. I was completely carried away and we made love without hesitation.

When it was over, I felt as though I had suddenly recovered from a strange dream and began to fully realize my lapse in judgment. The weight of his body next to mine felt awkward. I wanted my bed back to myself as soon as possible, and luckily, he made preparations to leave without any prompting. Before he left, he took down my telephone number and email address.

I did wonder the next morning if I'd ever hear from him again, or whether I needed to find another restaurant. My head felt heavier than usual, and I blamed alcohol for my predicament. When I finally left my bed and started my computer, I discovered he had already emailed me and said he was hoping to see me again soon.

※　※　※

Of course, nothing is without complications. Troy lives with a woman—has for nearly a decade, in effect making her his common-law wife. In my self-help books, this situation would be referred to as an attraction to "emotionally unavailable men." While I'm certain that this is a tale that women have been falling for since we learned to walk upright, I'm inclined to believe Troy when he says that his relationship is merely one of convenience, long since bereft of a sexual connection. They bought a condominium together when prices were better, and now neither of them wants to give it up, so they are locked into permanent roommate status.

Looking at this objectively, I shake my head. Why am I embroiled in some affair with a short-order cook with a girlfriend at home? What could possibly be in this for me, other than the inevitable heartbreak? But here I am, mooning over him like some lovesick schoolgirl.

I will tell you what the secret is. It is what happens in the bedroom. He is the most unusual lover I have ever had, and the reactions he provokes in me are strange and compelling. For example, he talks to me during sex, in a manner that is reminiscent of the limited pornography I've viewed in my lifetime. He says things that no man has ever said to me before. Things that if I heard someone calling a woman in public would make me consider phoning the police. But when he breathes this filth into my ear while touching me just so, I am reduced to a compliant, aching mess. Sometimes he makes me say things back to him. It pains me to no end; I can feel every fibre of myself resisting, but he does not let up. He keeps insisting, often while I am on the very brink of climax, and then I do say them, I have no choice but to say them, and as soon as I do, the relief and release is profound. It is a kind of freedom that I have never felt before.

And then, in the aftermath, there is the calm of resting my head against his broad warm chest and feeling utterly spent and safe. Feeling as though I have nothing to hide. It has become rather addictive, I confess. Not just in terms of the sexual pleasure it brings me, which is enormous, but also the surprises about myself that I feel I am about to discover. I am a little afraid, as it seems the proverbial envelope is pushed every time we are together, and I don't want it to go too far. Perhaps the novelty will wear off soon enough and I'll be able to return to my life. Although why I am in a hurry to get back to that old misery, I'm not exactly sure. I've been eating and sleeping well; I am filled with nervous energy and excitement. I have what could be described as a spring in my step.

✳   ✳   ✳

One of the things I enjoy most about Troy is that I don't feel as though I'm pretending when I'm with him. I seem to have lost the need to lie, to present a false self. I certainly can't tell any lies in the bedroom, and it doesn't seem worth it to tell them anywhere else. Of course, I'm aware of the irony, since the very nature of our affair is concealment.

Troy understands the person I am, sometimes in ways that I think might be more accurate than the ways in which I know myself. Last night in bed, he flipped me over and began spanking me while working my cunt over with his other hand. "That's it, that's my good girl," he said over and over, and I joined in the chorus. After I orgasmed, I became a crying, blubbering heap. He gathered me in his arms and held me while I sobbed, then lifted my face to his and asked me sweetly, "If you're a good girl, then what am I?"

"You're my daddy," I whispered. It came from me without thought or hesitation. But recounting it now, I am filled with shame. This shame mixes with my erotic memories of the moment and leaves me feeling very confused indeed.

❀ ❀ ❀

I know how foolish it is to hang my romantic hopes on this person. He is seldom able to stay the night, leaving me alone in my bed. I wonder why it matters to his wife that he comes home at all. (I have taken to calling her the "wife" in my mind because it's easier and it eliminates the trite, teenaged sound that "girlfriend" makes. If anyone gets that youthful moniker, I surmise, it ought to be me.) I want to ask questions about their relationship, yet I don't want to know the answers. I wonder what she looks like, if she is more attractive than me. Troy seems so committed to me and to our happiness. It is not surprising that when I ask questions, he brushes them aside. I imagine it's not something he wants to think about when we are enjoying our time together. When we are apart, we are always thinking of each other. He sends me text messages and emails at all hours of the day and night.

I long to please him sexually, and wonder what kinds of things we'll do next. I wonder if he gets tired of doing things the way we do, if sometimes he doesn't want things to be simpler and more "normal." But perhaps this is what "normal" is for Troy. I ask him about it, and he says he's had plenty of what he calls "vanilla" sex. "But I could tell you needed something more." He tells me that women have always been drawn to him for that, that he's found himself in this role before, and that he enjoys it. I feel an ache of envy even thinking about others. Were they better than me? Did they enjoy practices even more outrageous? Did he care for them the way I believe he cares for me? But I say nothing. I would rather not ask than run the risk of being lied to.

❋   ❋   ❋

He has a magnificent cock. He fucks me so perfectly with it, with an understanding of timing and restraint that I've never experienced in another man. That waiting, that holding back, is half the battle. I feel like a fool, but the force of my emotions and the power of my orgasms often move me to tears. They are transporting. Sometimes when I climax, he has to hold me up around my waist while tears and fluid and wails and sobs pour out of me. He holds me in his strong arms and kisses me tenderly and calls me "babe." How can I not love him?

❋   ❋   ❋

Since I've been spending so much of my free time online, waiting for messages from Troy, I've taken to doing a bit of internet research on my recent sexual interests. Beyond the ridiculous photographs and the least-erotic texts I've ever read, there are a number of serious discussion groups and forums for women to have intelligent conversations on the subject. I joined one of these groups in the hopes of finding some like-minded individuals. I cannot believe that I'm suddenly a part of an online BDSM chat group. It turns out that this acronym, that I assumed stood for Bondage, Domination, and Sadomasochism, is actually more of a catch-all term for Bondage and Discipline, Domination and Submission, and Sadism and Masochism. According to my research, I am a Submissive. Good heavens. Only months ago, I would have assumed that anyone involved in such a thing was a fringe-dweller in need of psychotherapy. On another site, I discovered a checklist of practices and sexual activities that partners could peruse together. I also read about things like "safe words", which is the BDSM way of saying "uncle" in a world where shrieking "no" is all part of the fun, and "soft limits", which are things that you wouldn't want to do if left to your own devices, but might be willing to do in service to a master. I bookmarked the list and showed it to Troy on his next visit. He did point out a few things he had done before, and I felt again the hot-cheeked, irrational envy of a teenager. There were a number of items and activities on the list I didn't even understand, and dozens in which I had no interest. I felt embarrassed by my pedestrian desires.

❋   ❋   ❋

I washed Troy's feet in a basin beside the couch while he watched *Family Guy* (a program more punishing to my sensibilities than any spanking) and then dried them with my hair. He's asked that I stop cutting it. I have gained three pounds this week, and now, when he comes over, one of our foreplay activities is my "weigh-in." I don't feel any particular erotic charge from my increasing size, but anything that I know will lead to sex is exciting enough. I feel rather glamorous about it all, like some kind of showgirl in reverse. And my slacks are no longer falling off my hips.

❋   ❋   ❋

My face is pressed so deeply into the pillow that I struggle to get any air at all. I arch against the strain of the cuffs, my arms bound behind my back and shackled to my ankles, my legs folded beneath me. There comes a point where fear takes over, leading to panic and more thrashing, and the tenor turns abruptly away from sex. One loses control over responses or emotions when the prevailing thought becomes "please don't let me die." And yet, underneath it all still is this strange and wonderful undercurrent of desire, this yearning and throbbing sensation throughout the body that is so much life in the midst of possible death.

Just as I am convinced I'm going to lose consciousness, Troy yanks my head up from the pillow by my ponytail and I draw a delicious cool and shuddering breath. It is, I imagine, what nearly drowning feels like, to get one's bearings back and kick towards the light until finally breaking the surface of the water. As I'm still gasping, Troy pulls out of me, rolls me onto my side and drags me towards the edge of the bed, where he fucks my open mouth and I pant and puff through my nose. I taste my own cunt before he takes his cock in his hand and, groaning, directs his semen over my face, thoughtfully avoiding my eyes, since I like to watch.

This is sex as true union, I have discovered. I think back to all of my previous sexual experiences, of boredom and faked orgasms. Certainly, having a new partner was entertaining and novel, and that often provided a kind of thrill, but it was a thrill borne solely of anxiety, not of trust. The times I lay there imagining a former experience or some fantasy image, instead of feeling a true union with my lover. Everything was built around the idea of achieving orgasm, which, while not an unworthy goal, does miss the point somewhat. What a joy it is to discover orgasm as an inevitable part of the journey, a glorious destination created in trust and in letting go. The sex act offers the promise of union, but I had seldom felt anything akin to true oneness before Troy. The ridiculous notion that a woman's vagina was some kind of physical portal to romantic ecstasy, an opening to a spectral plane—how outmoded and patriarchal, I reasoned, especially when I had taken lovers into this supposedly intimate place and still was able to contemplate my to-do list, or craft clever stories to tell about the experience later.

But pain! Pain is unifying. Pain leaves no room for to-do lists or anything else. When my face is in the pillow and my limbs are tightly bound, there's precious little room for thought. There is only feeling, and a kind of prayer that I will be rescued from this bondage, this prison of my own making. It is then that I am at one with Troy, that I give over, quite literally, my life to him. This is the ecstasy; this is that spectral plane. I am alone still, perhaps, but alive. Aware. Present.

❋   ❋   ❋

I have trouble with some of the terminology in "the scene" and wonder how much of it is necessary. Master and slave make me cringe, for obvious reasons. Dominant and submissive are more accurate, but clinical. Top and bottom seem to be the exclusive province of the gay community. Some women call their partners "Sir." That, at least, strikes me as elegant. Troy's nickname for me is D.W. It stands for Dirty Whore, which amuses.

❋   ❋   ❋

Although my work skirts still fit, I've taken to exclusively wearing long sleeves and slacks to the office. Despite our best efforts to be cautious, sometimes bruises find their way onto my arms and legs and neck. A couple of my coworkers have asked if I'm all right. I seem distracted, they say, or sad, and they don't want to pry, but they are worried about me. It's a peculiar thing, because I feel more energized and elated than ever before. I suppose to the outside observer, I might seem quieter, even sullen, but that is simply the result of having stripped away the lies and the falsehoods from my life. Now that I understand what love really is, I don't have a lot to say unless it's important. There was a time when these people, these strangers, really, had so much influence over my life. I wanted them to like me, to respect me. Now I discover I don't care what they think of me or my life, and so I suppose I have been gradually writing them out. I spend more and more time on the forums with the women who understand what I'm experiencing right now, and who live the life that I long to live, as many of them are lucky enough to be married to their Sirs.

❋　❋　❋

Electrical tape created a bold contrast with my pale flesh. Each tightly tape-encircled breast first turned red, then purple. My weight gain has made my breasts larger, which pleases Troy. He beat them with the flat side of my hairbrush until my left nipple began to bleed. At first I felt the pain, then realized I was too numb to feel it at all. It's interesting how so much of what one interprets as pain is simply a reaction to the visual feedback of injury. Troy licked the blood away, then pushed me into a kneeling position on the floor. He stood and, gathering my hair in one hand and lifting my face to him, smacked me over and over across the face with his erection. I shifted my weight enough to grind my clitoris against my right heel, as we came together, me against my foot and Troy on my bruised and bleeding breasts. It was marvelous.

❋　❋　❋

I want to disappear into this world. I want to belong to him utterly, to be lost in him and serve his every desire. I long to feel the freedom of giving in completely, to the complete sublimation of my own needs. I assume this is the draw of the cult, the fervor of the religious fanatic. My god is sex and pain and all I want to do is pray.

❋　❋　❋

Troy cornered me in the entranceway and checked to make sure I wasn't wearing any panties. I was nervous, with it being such a stupidly short skirt, but I didn't dare disobey him. In the restaurant, he took his steak knife under the table and ran the tip along my thigh. I tried to look at ease as I gulped back red wine. On the way home, we cut through the park, and he led me over to a bench. Troy finger-fucked me while some old drunk watched us from the other side of the baseball diamond. On the walk home, my exposed thighs gleamed wet under the streetlights.

✳   ✳   ✳

Troy and I had casually discussed the possibility of inviting another woman for a threesome, but when Troy texted me that he'd found someone and they were both on their way over, I felt more than a little panicked. I wished I'd had more time to clean, as one does, but tried not to fret. I suppose some of my anxiety about tidiness was more about my having sex with a woman, something I'd never done. I turned down the lights, lit some candles, and threw the laundry in the closet. I had approximately forty minutes. Grand Marnier was the only liquor in the cupboard, so I had a couple quick swallows. I didn't want to look as though I was trying too hard, but I did change into my cream silk nightgown and pulled my hair back. I also put on my faux pearl choker, thinking Troy might like to drag it through our labia later.

The woman, Sherry, was beautiful—certainly prettier than me. She was an excellent guest, arriving with a bottle of Shiraz, which I promptly uncorked. I have never been so grateful for a glass of wine. We worked our way through the bottle quickly, making awkward small talk. Troy took our empty glasses from us and we walked into the bedroom and sat on the bed. Sherry and I began kissing. I was amazed at how soft she was; her skin was like velvet and she smelled of baby-powder-scented antiperspirant and hairspray, but in the most pleasant way. Her mouth was full and soft on me. I understood how men could drive themselves mad over such softness, such tastes and smells. It was easily the most vanilla intercourse Troy and I had had in a very long time, but there was no shortage of novelty that night, thanks to Sherry's presence.

Although I enjoyed myself, I'm not sure I'd want to repeat the performance. There was a single moment that night that keeps playing in my memory. Troy was directing traffic, as it were, and when he was asking

Sherry to move over to the other side of the bed, he said tenderly, "C'mere, babe." I know I shouldn't dwell on it, and that it probably means nothing, but it stung worse than any slap. I'm having extraordinary difficulty letting it go.

❈   ❈   ❈

Sometimes I am troubled by what I read online. My new acquaintances in the BDSM community are, for the most part, articulate, well rounded, and intelligent. I don't always agree with them, but I appreciate their candor. But occasionally I read about some woman's journey into this lifestyle and wonder if what she's doing is simply being complicit in her own oppression. Sometimes I have felt as though I want to turn my entire life over to Troy, but then I discover that some women have done exactly that. Their partners make all the decisions about their lives, and the woman works and raises the children and is then expected to have her master-created list of chores completed before he returns home, or risk real punishment. Sometimes the power and pain is restricted to the bedroom, while others are collared and shackled, or have to sit on the floor, even for meals. I try not to judge their choices, but I can't help but contemplate the line between submission and victimization. Is there a difference between being dominated and being abused? And where does all of this leave me?

❈   ❈   ❈

In my spare time, I've taken to writing all these confused and jumbled feelings down. I spend so much time online and I've posted some of my ramblings in the BDSM forums. I put in some line breaks, and I know that these "poems" are just dreadful, but they help me organize the chaos in my mind. The response from readers has been tremendously encouraging, which is kind.

"Make it New"
To make it new means what?
To begin again, to be born again?
To be redeemed and
clean at last?
Pain is my redeemer
pain is my meditation
pain is emptiness and reception.
I am the vessel through
which the divine can be glimpsed.
There is a place where it is new
it is a place beyond sex
but you have to go through sex to get there.

I post this as I'm waiting for Troy to send me a message. I want to believe what I've written, but it rings false. I even extracted a line that was about being stripped of one's worries and one's consciousness. That was too much of a lie, even for me. My bruises, even as I sit nursing them with arnica ointment and cool compresses, are just a distraction. My worries and my consciousness are still very much present. It could be argued that I have just as many problems in my life as I did before I met Troy, and I've merely gotten better at ignoring them. In fact, if the last few days are any indication, I have even more to be concerned about. Here I am, battered and bruised, waiting for some man to instant-message me. I hardly see anyone outside this relationship, the relationship itself is an affair, my co-workers are worried about my sanity, I sneak around my own city going to strange restaurants so we won't be caught, and my body looks like I've been pushed down a flight of stairs. I don't feel free of anything.

❀　　❀　　❀

When I think about Troy, I realize that I know very little about him beyond what I've experienced of him directly. His expressions of love and fidelity are meaningless, really. Who's to say he doesn't go home to his wife and make love to her after seeing me, or any other number of women? I was so flattered by his attentions, by my own pampered vanity, that I ignored his guarded nature. I was only interested in how he saw me, and the potential to become a new person in his eyes. The further we go in this relationship, the more I see that this…thing that we have, cannot solely sustain me. It's as though I barely know him outside the bedroom. When I try to think of us talking, or walking together, I can't quite picture him. If Troy's not hitting me or fucking me, then what is he? He becomes formless, ghostly.

❋   ❋   ❋

The wife went out of town to visit relatives and Troy invited me back to his apartment after dinner. I eagerly accepted, thinking only of how much I would learn about him there, how I would finally see where he spent his time away from me. On the trip over, however, I began to have doubts. There were certain to be things there that I didn't want to see, symbols and souvenirs of a couple who'd spent more than ten years together. It also occurred to me that Troy would most likely want to have sex there. My initial excitement turned to dread, my chest tight with anxiety.

Once inside his condo, my eyes ran wild, scanning the rooms and taking in as much information as I could. Gathering clues, I suppose. The apartment was generic in style, the usual assortment of furnishings from low-priced chain stores; an enormous flat-screen television dominated the living room. It was clean and relatively tidy, save for an assortment of magazines and DVDs scattered on the coffee table. In the kitchen, a single pot sat soaking in the sink. A water glass on the kitchen counter. On a bookshelf, a photograph of Troy and a woman on top of a mountain somewhere. He was considerably thinner and smiling. She was blonde and chesty, but in an outdoorsy rather than a glamorous way. She had large, even teeth.

We sat on the leather sofa together and I feigned interest in a travel magazine. Troy asked if I wanted to watch a movie and I agreed, relieved to have something else to think about.

"I hope you like it," he said, grinning back at me. He slid a VHS cassette into a VCR on the bottom shelf of the entertainment unit.

"You still have a VCR?" I asked, incredulous and laughing. "What on earth are we watching?"

After a few moments of grey fuzz, a grainy image flickered to life on the screen. An Asian woman stood before the camera in a white bra and underwear. She said something I couldn't make out, and then laughed. She bent down and removed her panties, her long dark hair hanging in front of her face. She took off her bra, and spun around with her arms overhead. I heard a man's voice in the background. It was Troy. Then I realized I recognized the setting; they were in his living room.

There was an abrupt cut—in the next instant, the woman was bent over the couch and Troy was fucking her from behind. The colours of their skin stood out against the black leather. She whimpered with each thrust. I closed my eyes.

Troy touched my hand and I jumped. He looked at me. "Well?" he asked. "What do you think?"

"I don't know. Who is she?"

"It's from a long time ago," he said consolingly. "Way before your time, babe. I thought maybe we could make a newer one." He put his arm around me and lifted my chin to kiss me.

I slid away. "I'm not doing this."

"What do you mean?" He looked confused. "Take off your panties, but leave your skirt on. Do it slowly."

"I'm being serious, Troy. I can't do this, not here." I scanned the room for a video camera, but saw none.

"I thought we might go to the bedroom instead, since it's more comfortable…" He pulled me close to him again and buried his face in my hair, whispering in a way that usually sent shudders through me. "It's okay, babe, it's okay, nothing bad's going to happen, I promise."

I shook my head against his shoulder, ignored the husky voice in my ear. "No, I mean it. Nothing bad is going to happen because I'm not doing this. I want to go home." I stood up.

"Why are you being like this?"

"Why do you think?" I glanced at the woman on the screen, who now held an impressive length of Troy's cock in her mouth. I put my head down and made for the door. I didn't want to see anything else. I knew if I stayed for one more minute, Troy would cajole me and I would give in. I knew that with just a few more words of persuasion and gentle caresses, I'd be lying in the bed that he and the chesty blonde slept in together every night. The smell of her on the sheets. And her, or some other woman, watching me make love on video one day. This was my soft limit, a level of pain I wasn't ready to reach.

Troy was furious but insisted on taking me home. He said nothing on the drive back to my place, his face tight and ruddy. I exited the car without a word from either of us. Something in me felt rebellious and righteous, and although it wasn't sex, it felt good anyway. I was certain I'd be paying for it later.

❋   ❋   ❋

During play, it didn't feel exceptionally hard when Troy struck me, but I've come to discover that my own assessment of pain is wildly changeable and inaccurate when I'm in "subspace."

Afterwards, he looked at my face and winced. "You'd better go look in the mirror." The shape of his fingers was unmistakably printed on my cheek in stripes of red and white.

Upon rising the next morning, I examined my reflection while brushing my teeth. The imprint of Troy's hand was still there. Less red certainly, but still visible, and joining it was a pool of congealing darkness under my left eye. I pulled out my limited arsenal of makeup to try and disguise it, but my equipment and experience were lacking and the resulting camouflage job was cakey, obvious, and largely ineffective. I left my hair down in an attempt to cover some of my face, but I looked a wreck. But I couldn't afford to miss the day's work—in addition to having no sick days left for the year, I also had an important meeting to attend.

❋　❋　❋

All morning I observed people around the office looking at me strangely, but I kept my eyes down and pretended not to notice. One new hire asked me what happened, but I fixed her with a cold stare that sent her scampering to the lunchroom without another word. Back at my desk, I got a call from my boss's admin assistant, asking me to come by Linda's office at my earliest convenience.

Linda didn't waste any time. "What happened to your face, Susanna?"

"I hurt myself," I replied too brightly, as though I were a child proud of a boo-boo.

"I want you to know I'm concerned." In her voice I could hear a warning. "Your behaviour has been rather…unusual lately," she said. She glanced at some papers on her desk as though they were the source of additional information. "You've been calling in sick, missing deadlines… If there's a personal issue, we're here to help."

"No, no issue," I said. I could see in her face that I wasn't getting away so easily. "Well, there have been some problems," I added tentatively, and sure enough, she leaned forward for the scoop. "It's just…" I drew a long breath, as though the terrible truth was about to pour out of me.

"Yes?" she asked too eagerly.

"Well," I said, taking the out, "it's not something I can really talk about at the moment. I just needed a little time, but things are getting better now." Linda leaned back again, clearly disappointed.

"I'm glad to hear it."

"As am I. I can assure you, Linda, I won't be giving anyone further cause for alarm."

"Good, good..." she trailed, her mind already switching gears to the next item on her agenda. "Well, do keep me posted," she added, standing to signal the end of the conversation.

"Oh, I will," I said, smiling.

"One more thing?"

"Yes?"

"Why don't you take the rest of the afternoon? I'll email you the notes from the meeting and we'll see you tomorrow."

And as I walked through the door of Linda's office and past the desks and the meeting rooms and the reception area and out the door, it occurred to me that I had meant what I said. That I was done with the whole sordid business. For the first time in my life, the truth was far more scandalous than any lie I could invent, and yet, I could tell no one. I was exhausted.

※　※　※

What is there that is left to say? There was resistance, tears, shouting, and second thoughts from both parties. Flowers were delivered to my home, to my workplace. A lapse in judgment found Troy back in my bed, just once. I immediately contracted a yeast infection so pernicious I initially feared venereal disease. I listened to songs about broken hearts, unsubscribed from my internet forums without a goodbye, and got a decent haircut at a chic downtown salon. I put in extra hours at the office and spent my lunch hours in the gym, running on a treadmill until sweat ran into my eyes. I stood in my bedroom filling a box with items undonatable to any reputable thrift shop: a rubber dress, fleece-lined wrist and ankle cuffs, nipple clamps, a neon-orange butt plug, a leather-wrapped paddle. I sealed the box with what was left of the black electrical tape and pushed it to the back of the closet. I had become a woman with a past, with a proper secret.

✵   ✵   ✵

Am I happy? I'm not convinced I'd go so far as to call it that. But I eat and sleep and work and make it through each day feeling as though something's been accomplished. I telephone my mother and father once a week. I contribute to my RRSP. I'm thinking of painting my living room a colour I saw in a magazine. I purchase toilet paper and toothpaste in bulk at Costco, and once, I saw Troy and his wife there. I peered from behind a lineup of people clamouring for cake samples and watched the two of them picking out patio furniture together. I waited for grief or anxiety to take hold of me, but I didn't feel anything close to heartsick. They looked pleased with their eventual selection. I couldn't even remember if they had a balcony, which seemed strange, given how I would have clamored for such information less than a year ago. The person I was then seemed like someone from another lifetime. It felt rather like those instances when I've caught sight of myself in a strangely angled window. I see a woman and that woman is me, but in that unexpected moment, I do not recognize her at all.

ACKNOWLEDGMENTS

An earlier version of "Blonde" appeared in issue 54/55 of *subTerrain* magazine. "Day of the Dead" appeared in the summer 2010 issue of *Forget* magazine (Vol. 5, Issue 3).

I would like to express my gratitude to the Canada Council for the Arts, The British Columbia Arts Council, and The Banff Centre for their generous support of this project.

This book owes much to the editorial guidance and feedback from mentors and peers at The Banff Centre's Writing Studio program, and to the literary festivals and events that provided the opportunity to shape and share works in progress: the Galiano Island Literary Festival, Hamilton's GritLIT festival, Vancouver's Word on the Street, and the W2 Real Vancouver Writers series.

I am indebted to the wonderful Katie Pretti for allowing me to reproduce her piece, "Untitled (Splitting) 1", on the book's cover.

Finally, heartfelt thanks to Brian at Anvil Press for his patience and support, and to Rob, who picks up the red pen only when forced, and then with much kindness.